World
Made of
Glass

ALSO BY AMI POLONSKY

Threads

Gracefully Grayson

World
Made of
Glass

Ami Polonsky

LITTLE, BROWN AND COMPANY

New York   Boston

Copyright © 2023 by Ami Polonsky

Cover art copyright © 2023 by Ileana Soon.
Cover design by Patrick Hulse. Cover copyright © 2023 by Hachette Book Group, Inc.

Little, Brown and Company
Hachette Book Group
1290 Avenue of the Americas, New York, NY 10104
Visit us at LBYR.com

First Edition: January 2023

Little, Brown and Company is a division of Hachette Book Group, Inc. The Little, Brown name and logo are trademarks of Hachette Book Group, Inc.

The publisher is not responsible for websites (or their content) that are not owned by the publisher.

Little, Brown and Company books may be purchased in bulk for business, educational, or promotional use. For information, please contact your local bookseller or the Hachette Book Group Special Markets Department at special.markets@hbgusa.com.

Library of Congress Cataloging-in-Publication Data
Names: Polonsky, Ami, author.
Title: World made of glass / Ami Polonsky.
Description: First edition. | New York : Little, Brown and Company, 2023. | Audience: Ages 10–14. | Summary: "Iris opens her eyes to hard truths and the power of her voice when her father dies of AIDS in 1987"—Provided by publisher.
Identifiers: LCCN 2022007802 | ISBN 9780316462044 (hardcover) | ISBN 9780316462259 (ebook)
Subjects: CYAC: Fathers—Fiction. | Grief—Fiction. | AIDS (Disease)—Fiction | Prejudices—Fiction. | LCGFT: Fiction.
Classification: LCC PZ7.P7687 Wo 2023 | DDC [Fic]—dc23
LC record available at https://lccn.loc.gov/2022007802

ISBNs: 978-0-316-46204-4 (hardcover),
978-0-316-46225-9 (ebook)

Printed in the United States of America

LSC-C

Printing 1, 2022

For Daniel, Ben, and Ethan

World Made of Glass

Chapter One

*D*ad. *Is. Dying.*

I pushed through the after-school crowd in the hallway, repeating the sentence to myself: *Dad. Is. Dying. Dad. Is. Dying.* With each word, I planted one of my hot-pink Converse into the center of a scuffed floor tile. *No stepping on cracks.* I didn't used to be the superstitious type, but these days, new worries popped into my mind constantly. Maybe repeating the thought over and over again would help me to understand it.

Dad. Is. Dying, and just this morning, Mom said it wouldn't be long now.

Dad. Is. Dying. The words pounded through my

mind on loop as I passed the lunchroom and nurse's office. Rounding the corner by the gym, I almost ran into Ms. Staffio. Startled, she hopped to the side to avoid me.

"Iris!" she exclaimed. I was probably imagining it, but she seemed disgusted, as if nearly bumping into me could contaminate her. Then she patted her already-neat bun. "Pay attention to where you're going, please." She forced a smile and adjusted the teacher's edition of our science textbook under her arm. "I was just on my way to make some photocopies, but I was hoping to see you. I wanted to ask you something."

I took one more step to complete my thought (*Dying.*) before responding. "'Kay," I said.

She looked at me strangely, and for a second, I thought I saw a flicker of something different in her eyes. Sympathy? But no. It couldn't be. Nobody, not even my best friends, knew that Dad was sick.

"You're off to Philanthropy Club, I presume?"

"Yeah," I answered.

"Wonderful. The gerbils' cage really could use a cleaning. Will you pass that along to the group? I mean, unless you have something *more* philanthropic on the agenda." I couldn't tell if she was being sarcastic.

Everyone knew that Philanthropy Club was the after-school activity you joined if your parents insisted that you "get involved" and you had nothing better to do.

Ms. Staffio smoothed her hair again and adjusted the already-perfect collar of her white blouse. Everything about her was so judgmental, and even though I'd gotten really good at not caring what people thought about me and my family, I wondered what was going through her mind.

That Iris, I imagined her thinking in her snooty tone, *she looks so disheveled. Someone ought to take her in for a bangs trim—her hair is dangling into her eyes. And on the topic of her eyes, why are they so droopy and bloodshot? It's like she hasn't slept in ages. Must be that odd family of hers. Must be because her dad is, you know . . . gay.* In my mind, she'd whisper the last word, *gay*, because it was so unthinkable.

Well, if those were Ms. Staffio's thoughts, she would have been right about my appearance. I hadn't been able to find my hairbrush that morning, and my bangs *were* hanging into my eyes because for weeks, everyone at home had been too distracted by Dad dying to take me to his barber on the corner for a bangs trim. And my eyes *were* bloodshot from not sleeping enough, because when your dad is sick, the nightmares claw at you until you wake up, and half of your mind is in your bedroom, and you're looking out your darkened, eighth-story window over Greenwich Village, dotted with streetlights and car lights and sometimes a two a.m. siren, but the other half of your brain has never seen this bedroom before. Has never seen a bedroom at all, actually. The window glass might not even be there, and it's probably not, and if you roll over, you'll be falling through eight stories of thin, too-cold March air to the sidewalk below.

"Iris!" Ms. Staffio said, as if it wasn't the first time she'd tried to get my attention.

"Yeah?" I asked. The perimeter around the tiles appeared to be shrinking. Moving closer to my shoes. I clenched and unclenched my toes.

"You'll clean out the gerbils' cage today? They're starting to stink. Extra garbage bags are in the cabinet."

"Oh yeah," I told her. "The gerbils. Sure."

She tilted her head to the side as if exhausted by our conversation, or at the very least, confused, and walked away.

I gave up stepping in the centers of the tiles.

In Mr. Inglash's room, Toby and Will were already at the back table. They were weird and annoying, and I loved hanging out with them. Being in the same room as my closest friends made the tightness in my stomach disappear. I allowed myself to forget about how condescending Ms. Staffio was as I joined them.

"No way," Toby was saying emphatically while wiping his always-stuffy nose with the back of his hand, his eyes wide with enthusiasm about whatever he and Will were debating. "There is *no way* that a half-eaten Charleston Chew with your slobber cooties all over it, a baggie of probably stale pretzels, and mini muffins are worth an unopened two-pack of SnoBalls. How gullible do you think I am?" He caressed, and then kissed, his package of pink Hostess SnoBalls.

"*Significantly* gullible," Will replied. "And can I point out that you're making out with your after-school snack?" he continued, grinning, as he leaned back in his chair and rested his shoes on the table next to his Charleston Chew. He poured the entire bag of mini muffins into his mouth and suppressed a cough.

Dad's sickness loosened its grip on my shoulders as I watched Will attempt to chew. Slobbery bits of muffin escaped his mouth, falling onto his lap. He picked them up one by one and poked them back between his clenched lips.

I pretended to gag. "I hope you know CPR and the Heimlich, Toby," I said, "because if he chokes, no way am I saving him."

"Hello to you, too," Toby said, wiping his nose on the back of his hand again. Will rocked back on his chair legs, waved, and continued chewing.

Grinning, I ran over to the classroom window and cranked it open. Cold March air tumbled in. "Mallory!" I screamed into the void. "Why did you have to move?" Toby, Will, and I laughed as a bunch of kids on the playground turned to look in my direction.

"I feel so sorry for you that she's in Philly now," Will said as I relatched the window. "Like, seriously, *seriously* sorry." He rubbed his buzz cut. Will was the only African American kid in our grade. Since becoming friends with him, Toby, and Mallory the year before, I'd wondered how he felt being one of the only kids at our private school who wasn't white, but that wasn't the kind of thing anyone ever talked about. So for now, I just wondered how he had managed to chew that entire package of mini muffins in one swoop without choking.

I smiled at him, glad that he hadn't needed the Heimlich over muffins. "Thanks," I told him. "I feel sorry for me, too." Mallory, the fourth seventh-grade misfit, former member of the Philanthropy Club, Dungeon Master, and my best friend, had moved to Philadelphia over winter break. We talked on the phone every Sunday after dinner, and I'd seen her a few times when she and her family had come into the city, but I couldn't bring myself to tell her that Dad was sick.

Toby ripped open his SnoBalls, pink coconut spilling onto the table, and motioned to one of them. "Go ahead," he said.

"Yes! Come to Papa," Will sang, pulling a SnoBall in two, handing one piece to me, and shoving his half into his mouth.

I licked the sugary pink coating off the white marshmallow exterior. I was usually able to forget about the whole dying thing for a while at Philanthropy Club, and I was pretty sure that Mom suspected this, which was likely why she still insisted that I go, even though what I really wanted to do after school was race home to Dad and J.R.'s apartment.

"Oh, Ms. Staffio wants us to clean the gerbils," I told Will and Toby.

"Clean the gerbils?" Toby asked, laughing, as he took a giant bite. Pink coconut stuck to the tip of his nose, and I wondered if his snot had served as glue.

"Hey," Will chimed in. "Do you have a toothbrush? We can lather the gerbils up in the science-room sink and scrub them with a toothbrush, and then put them in, like, little robes—"

"Did you just ask me if I had a toothbrush?" Toby interrupted. "Sure, I brought my toothbrush to school, and I want to use it to clean *Stiff*io's gophers."

Will cracked up. "*Gophers?*" he asked. "Man, they're *gerbils!*"

"What's the difference?" Toby asked, hopping up and grabbing the *G* encyclopedia from Mr. Inglash's bookshelf. I wandered back to the window, wishing again that Mallory were still here. I wondered, if she hadn't moved, would I finally be able to tell her about Dad? She wasn't the type to judge anybody, but still, I didn't know.

I licked sticky goo from my fingertips while peering out at the now-empty playground. Will's and Toby's voices faded into the background, and just like when I woke up from a nightmare, I was halfway in the real world and halfway disconnected.

"A gopher is a burrowing rodent with fur-lined pouches on the insides of its cheeks," Toby read. Outside the window, some of the dirty snow piles still lingered, like Manhattan didn't know whether it was winter or spring. I remembered being little, when it was just me, Mom, and Dad. Back before everything got so complicated. Mom and Dad loved each other then. *They still love each other*, I reminded myself.

A gust of wind shook the empty swings and rattled the windows as Toby went on. "Man, if I had little fuzzy pockets in my cheeks, that would be so awesome! I'd fill them with jawbreakers and nobody would ever know! Or Hot Pockets! Look up gerbils. I want to know if gerbils have furry mouth pockets." They both cracked up some more. Across the street was Gramercy Park, its trees just starting to bud, and beyond it, past Union Square, was NYU, where J.R. worked and where Dad used to, back before he got too sick to do anything.

"A gerbil is an old-world burrowing desert rodent," Toby read. "What the heck? An old-world rodent? Are Stiffio's gerbils time travelers?"

I turned back to Toby and Will, trying to smile. They could have gone on forever, talking about mouth pockets, Hot Pockets, rodents, and time travel. I wished I could care about that kind of stuff again.

I looked through the little window in the doorway to where Mr. Inglash was saying something to the top of some kid's head, but by the time he came in, the blond mop of hair had disappeared. "It's the philanthropic clubbers!" he announced, pushing his glasses up on his nose, the fluorescent lights bouncing off his shiny, bald head. He was the dorkiest and best teacher in the school. A while back, Mallory, Will, Toby, and I had made a banner that said 7TH-GRADE ENGLISH WITH INGLASH in bubble letters to hang above the blackboard. *That* was the type of philanthropy project we could manage. The sign was still there.

"What's on the agenda for the day?" Mr. Inglash went on. I liked that he took us seriously, even though we never had anything on our agenda beyond random projects and playing Dungeons & Dragons when we were done. It was almost like he was waiting for the day that we'd finally announce our plans to save the world. I was kind of waiting for that day, too.

"We're going to go clean Ms. Stiff"—I caught myself, and Mr. Inglash hid a smile—"Ms. *Staffio's* gophers. I mean, gerbils. I mean, not the animals. Their cage."

"Then we'll probably try to play DnD with a bad DM and only two players, which *definitely* isn't fun...," Toby chimed in as I glanced at the clock, no longer distracted by Will, Toby, and the Philanthropy Club. I wanted to get home to see how Dad was doing.

10

Mr. Inglash looked thoughtful for a minute. Then he pushed his glasses up onto his nose again. "I'll talk to Ms. Staffio for you," he said. "Skip the hamster cage for the day." Will, Toby, and I burst into laughter.

"Gerbil," Toby corrected, still laughing.

"Ah, yes. Gerbil. Iris?" he asked. "Help me out with something?" I looked at Will and Toby, shrugged, and joined him in the empty hallway, where afternoon sunbeams slanted through the windows.

"So," Mr. Inglash said sort of awkwardly once he closed the classroom door. "I'm just wondering—I mean—what I'm trying to say," he stammered, "is how are you doing?"

I saw myself reflected in his thick glasses and thought of how I imagined myself in Ms. Staffio's eyes. Mr. Inglash wasn't like her. He actually cared. Looking down, I noticed that I was standing on the edges of the floor tiles, and I adjusted my shoes so they weren't touching the cracks.

After Dad had found out that he had AIDS, I'd overheard him and Mom talking in his and J.R.'s apartment about whether they should let my teachers know that he was sick. "She'll need support," Mom had said curtly. I'd stopped outside the door, key in hand, and pressed my ear to the metal to listen. It had been this past September, which was near the end of Mom's angry phase and a full year after she and Dad had separated.

"They'll treat her like a leper," Dad had said with finality. Mom had probably agreed, so that was the end of that conversation. As far as I knew, nobody outside of Mom, Dad, my grandparents, J.R., and their new friend Bob knew that Dad had AIDS; nobody else knew that he was dying. Sure, people knew Dad was gay and that he and Mom had gotten divorced because of it at the beginning of sixth grade, and plenty of them cared way too much about that, but that was *their* problem, not mine.

"Iris?" Mr. Inglash prodded.

"Oh, I'm fine, I guess?"

Unless people at school had somehow found out? Why had Mr. Inglash pulled me into the hall to see how I was doing? I started to feel nauseous from that Sno-Ball. Marshmallows always made me feel sick.

You could talk to him about it, a small voice in my head told me. *He wouldn't treat you like an outcast. He's Mr. Inglash.* Suddenly, the thought of telling Mr. Inglash about Dad—about the AIDS and the dying— felt like such a relief. But before I could open my mouth, he began to speak again.

"Glad to hear that things are fine, Iris. That's real good. So listen, there's a new student. I thought you might see if he wanted to join the Philanthropy Club. He's kind of reluctant to get involved, and I'm trying to help him make some connections."

I closed my eyes for a second and envisioned the window beside my bed in the middle of the night. In my mind, the outside air was thick. Humid. The way the air in the hallway suddenly felt. There was no glass on the window. No screen. If I rolled over, I'd fall.

At the end of the hallway, the mop of curly hair reappeared. Beneath it was a boy. "I'll go talk to Ms. Staffio," Mr. Inglash said. "About the gerbils." For a minute, it seemed like he was going to pat me on the shoulder, but instead he clasped his hands behind his back. Then he disappeared around the corner.

I looked the new kid over as he approached. Mr. Inglash was right; the boy didn't seem to want to be in this nearly empty after-school hallway at three fifteen on a Thursday afternoon. His hands were stuffed into his blue jeans pockets, and he took his time walking over, like he might swerve at the last minute and head for the front doors instead.

But he didn't. "Hi," he said when he stopped in

front of me. His eyes were very blue, and despite every-thing terrible, I couldn't help noticing that he was kind of cute.

"Hey," I said, more self-consciously than I'd meant to.

"Hi," he said again, looking down at his feet.

I looked down at mine. They stood diagonally across the lines around the tiles, but I ignored the urge to move them. "I'm Iris."

"Julian."

I nodded, feeling suddenly awkward. "So Mr. Inglash said you might be interested in joining Phil—"

"Yeah, sure," Julian replied even before I could fin-ish the sentence.

I opened the classroom door. Inside, Will and Toby stood at opposite ends of a long table. Will held a sling-shot made of a forked tree branch and rubber band. It was his latest geeky "simple machine," which he insisted on calling a catapult, and he was preparing to use it to fling a pretzel into Toby's open mouth.

"Three, two, one, launch!" he yelled. The pretzel flew through the air, hit Toby on the forehead, and broke into pieces.

I glanced at Julian from the corner of my eye. He seemed to be suppressing a smile, and I couldn't tell what he was thinking. That we were dorks? That we were his kind of people?

I introduced him to Will and Toby.

"Where'd you move from?" Will asked, loading another pretzel into his slingshot.

"Most recently? Indiana," Julian said, but he looked away like he didn't want to talk about it, so I changed the subject.

"You play DnD?" I asked, wondering if he'd make a good DM.

"Yeah," he replied.

"Cool, what's your character?" Will wanted to know.

"Elven fighter."

"Would you say half a Charleston Chew, a baggie of pretzels, and a package of mini muffins are worth as much as two SnoBalls?" Toby asked, scooping up some pretzel pieces and tossing them into the garbage can.

Julian picked at his fingernails. "Definitely not." He squeezed out a half smile.

On the one hand, Julian's reluctance to talk made him seem way too cool for us. On the other hand, I had the sense that he was holding himself back from diving right into our nerdy conversations. Mom says that everyone assumes they're the only one with struggles but, in reality, we're all dealing with something. Julian's situation, whatever it was, felt like a relief. It was a visible reminder that there's something weird about all of us.

"Bombs away!" Will yelled, bringing my attention back to the classroom. He wiggled his eyebrows and launched a pretzel toward me and Julian.

We ducked as it sailed over our heads and broke against the wall. I turned to Julian. "Welcome to Philanthropy Club."

Chapter Two

Back home, I rode the elevator to the eighth floor. Mom was rarely home from work at the NYU Medical Center before six. Lately, ever since Dad had stopped getting out of bed, Bob, who also worked at the medical center, would come with her to check on him.

I unlocked the front door and immediately looked down. As expected, a folded piece of notebook paper awaited me on the welcome mat. A poem from Dad.

I picked it up, unfolded the paper, and smoothed it out. This acrostic was called "WHISPERWARM," the title scrawled across the top line. And even though

I wanted to read it, I had to spend some time pacing around the apartment before I could bring myself to.

Dad and I had an ongoing joke about acrostic poetry that had started back in second grade when I'd gotten an assignment to write an acrostic poem entitled "MOM" for Mother's Day. The teacher's example had been:

MOM

Marvelous!
Out of this world!
My friend!

Dad and I couldn't stop laughing about how ridiculous the poem was. The next day, he'd brought home some really old acrostics from his office in the English department at NYU. We'd decided that, while they were *less* ridiculous, they were still generally absurd.

The poems under the door started about a year and a half ago, shortly after Mom and Dad had told me that Dad was gay, they were getting divorced, and Dad and J.R. were moving into a one bedroom together on the twelfth floor. (*So I can still be near you, Iris*, Dad had explained.)

I remembered sitting at the dining room table, stunned, as Dad had explained that he'd always known he was gay, but that he'd met J.R. at work, and J.R. had helped him to finally feel okay about it.

"Dad and I still love each other," Mom had added, her eyes puffy and red. "Just in a different kind of way."

I'd been furious at both of them. For days, I'd refused to speak.

About a week later, once Dad had brought all his clothes and books up to his and J.R.'s tiny apartment, I'd gotten home from school to find a piece of paper waiting for me on the welcome mat. It was a poem entitled "ACROSTIC."

ACROSTIC *by Steven Cohen*
September 12, 1985

Across time and Earth, after the windstorm
    (or leafstorm or hailstorm) small
Creatures storm soil, each an earthworm
Returning home. Hopeful, they carry each other.
    Carry
On, down, where damp roots, sweet-smelling, wait.
    Even the

Stupidest form of poetry, the acrostic, can

Tell a story. Start with the beating heart.

I

Challenge you: Write me back?

Even though I'd been furious at Dad, I'd smiled, because I had understood why he'd written me an acrostic. He'd been trying to teach me a lesson about how even the most terrible-seeming things in the world can be made better if you just looked at them in the right way. I'd known this because, as Mom always said, Dad and I were two peas in a pod.

It had taken me a while to respond to him, but finally, I'd managed an acrostic entitled "NO," even though the fact that I'd decided to write it had basically been like saying yes. I could never be mad at Dad for long.

NO *by Iris Cohen*
September 20, 1985

Never getting

Over this.

Of course, he'd written another, and I'd written

back. Each weekday, a poem awaited me after school. On the weekends, they were there when I woke up.

Now "ACROSTIC" was the first poem in the navy binder where I kept all Dad's poems.

Looking back, I could see how Dad's acrostics had started as a way to help me get over the divorce. And I did. I got over all of it.

Except for J.R.

I finally forced myself to look at Dad's poem "WHIS-PERWARM." I knew how he had come up with the title. *Whisperwarm* was a word from Anastasia Krupnik's famous poem, the one that her terrible teacher gave her an F on in the first Anastasia book by Lois Lowry. Dad and I had read all the books in the series together. We loved that they were about a girl whose dad was a professor of literature at a university, because that was our life, too. As I glanced over the poem, I couldn't help noticing that Dad's handwriting was getting lighter and lighter, as if holding a pen was becoming too hard for him.

I closed my eyes for a minute and imagined Dad lying in the hospital bed in the living room approximately forty feet above me. I flashed to my glassless bedroom window again. Rolling over in my sleep. Falling. Then I opened my eyes and read the poem.

WHISPERWARM *by Steven Cohen*

March 19, 1987

When you came into this world I

Held you

In a blanket until you

Seeped (colorful) through fabric, landed,

    sure-footed, solid,

Purposeful, by my side. You grew.

Every sidewalk was for hopscotch, every sky was for

Rainbows, each fountain for

Wishing. Whisper warm, Iris.

Apples with mint leaves.

Rambling ramiferous rivers.

Mud beneath your nails.

Dad always says that to write a poem, you first have to identify the beating heart of what you want to say. You have to see the heart, and hear it, and hold it in your hands, and then, once you've done all of that, you can write around that heart. Even though I'd have to look up *ramiferous*, I knew right away that the heart of this poem was me—*my* heart. Or at least the heart I used to have before Dad got sick.

In my bedroom, I snapped Dad's poem into the

binder and thought about the glass paperweights that he and I had picked out at the Corning Museum of Glass up by the Finger Lakes several years ago. Dabs and swirls of color spun inside them, like entire worlds, and I'd always thought of those paperweights as our hearts. They used to be on top of his messy stacks of papers on his desk at NYU, but since he had gotten too sick to work and had left his job, I hadn't seen them. I wondered where they were.

I took out a pencil and opened my binder, trying to visualize the beating heart of my response to Dad's poem. But each time I got close to something that felt real and true, I had to turn away, because the real and true thing didn't look anything like the magical swirls and drips of colors within a glass orb. The real and true thing was so gigantic and empty and freezing cold that I couldn't stand to be near it.

So I didn't even try to write him a poem. I just closed the binder and left.

The elevator always took forever, so I took the stairs to Dad and J.R.'s. Their front door was unlocked. I wanted to see Dad, but I didn't want to see Dad, so I pushed it open slowly. The truth was that Dad barely looked like himself anymore, and as soon as I walked into the apartment and saw him lying on the hospital bed in the corner of the living room, I felt the skin tugging at the sides of my chin like I was going to cry. But I forced myself not to.

"Hey, Earthworm," he whispered, weakly lifting his oxygen mask away from his face when he spoke.

I sat next to him on the bed and tried to smile, but when the side of my leg touched his through the crisp, white sheet, I flinched at his boniness.

"Hey, Iris," J.R. said from the kitchen doorway, which was just a few steps away from where I was sitting. J.R. was always gentle with me; he never made me talk. I got the feeling that he was going to wait for me to come around, even if coming around took a lifetime.

It made me hate him even more.

"Did you wash up yet?" he asked.

Mom and Bob were constantly reminding us to wash our hands, since Dad's immune system was shot and we didn't want to introduce new germs into the mix. I went to the kitchen sink and lathered my hands for a long time in warm water. Then J.R. handed me a plate of cut-up apples arranged in the shape of a flower with a blob of peanut butter in the center. And because

24

J.R. was J.R., the apples were sprinkled with green shreds of something or other.

I picked one of the green bits off an apple and smelled it. "Fresh mint," J.R. told me, smiling like he wanted me to be happy, and also like he'd understand if I threw my snack, including the ceramic plate, right into the trash. I thought of Dad's poem—*Apples with mint leaves*—and wondered which had come first, the poem or J.R.'s apples. I vowed, again, to work my hardest to hate him forever.

Nodding in thanks, I took the snack to Dad's bed. "Want a bite?" I asked, sitting down by his side, dipping a mint-sprinkled apple slice into peanut butter.

"A tiny one," he whispered back. I could tell that he didn't really want to eat. He just wanted me to think he did. He lifted his oxygen mask again and, suppressing a cough, took the tiniest nibble off the end. A part of me wanted to put it back on my plate. Everyone who understands anything about AIDS knows that you can't catch it through casual contact or even swapping spit with someone, but despite that, Dad wouldn't let me eat stuff that his mouth had been on. It made no sense, and he even agreed that it was irrational. But I didn't argue today; I just put the mostly whole apple slice on his bedside table.

"For later," I told him, even though we both knew

that someone—probably J.R.—would eventually throw it away. These days, Dad was living off weird-smelling concoctions, and even then, as soon as he'd take a sip, he'd just cough and cough.

I poked a sliver of mint leaf into an apple slice with my fingernail until it disappeared into pale yellow flesh. Then I looked back at Dad. His thinness and the purple splotchy things on his arms—they were hard to look at. But the hardest thing to see was his face. He was so skinny that his now-dull eyes seemed to have sunken lower than was humanly possible. You could see the shape of his skull beneath his skin.

He must have sensed my gaze. "I don't look so good, huh?" he whispered.

I looked down at my hands. "You've looked better, I guess."

"Sorry, Earthworm."

"It's not your fault, Dad."

J.R. was watching us from the kitchen doorway again, and he looked away when I said that.

The purple spots had started to appear on Dad's forehead and lower back this past winter. Kaposi's sarcoma. It was cancer that was caused by HIV. And Dad had it, and now pneumocystis pneumonia, too, which was going to

26

kill him, and J.R. was frying meatballs for the pasta sauce, and I wished that everything were reversed—that J.R. was the one sick and dying in bed while Dad made dinner. Then I hated myself for thinking that, because I despised J.R., but that didn't mean that I wanted him to die.

Dad took my hand. Squeezed it weakly. I thought of the whisperwarm and what I would do when whispers and warmth became quiet and cold. Then I rested my head on the pillow next to Dad's, closed my eyes, and listened to the sounds of his breathing.

I must have dozed off for a while, because I awoke to a soft knock on the door and the sound of the evening news. Dad's rattling breath quivered steadily next to me; he was asleep.

Mom and Bob came in, Mom still in her scrubs because it was Thursday, which was one of the days that she delivered babies, and Bob in his suit because he was a hospital administrator. He handed a brown paper lunch bag to J.R., who thanked him, and then he and Mom washed up.

"Were you sleeping, Nose-ris?" Bob asked, tousling my hair. He thought he was really clever, replacing the *I* in my name with other body parts as if my name were "Eye-ris." But I didn't mind. If you were in the right mood, Bob could be funny, in an extremely dorky kind of way.

"Yeah, I think I dozed off for a bit."

"More nightmares last night?" Mom asked as she gently lifted Dad's wrist to take his pulse. I knew better than to answer while she counted to herself.

"I guess," I admitted once she'd finished.

"Dinner's ready," J.R. announced, carrying a steaming pot to the cluttered table, which was meant for two people, not four. I sat in my usual spot on the end of Dad's bed, which nearly touched the table because the apartment was so small.

It's the only one in the building that's available, Dad had said when he'd told me about it. *Plus J.R. and I would live in a place the size of a shoebox before moving farther away from you.* I looked down at my plate now as I thought about it.

J.R. and I.

Had J.R. really been a part of that decision? Or did he just go along with it because he loved Dad?

"Look! Here it is," J.R. said suddenly, hopping up from his folding chair and adjusting the volume on the TV. The banner across the screen read *New drug approved to treat*

28

HIV and AIDS. A wave of hope rushed through me like the explosion of colors in one of Dad's paperweights.

"Mom!" I whispered, looking at her and then back to the TV.

"Good evening and hello from WABC in New York City. I'm Bill Beutel, and this is *Eyewitness News*," the anchor said. "It's Thursday, March nineteenth, 1987. Today the Federal Drug Administration approved the drug AZT for the treatment of HIV and AIDS." His voice sounded gray and flat as he spoke, not swirly pink and purple pastel like I felt inside. The screen shifted to a group of people chanting outside a building under a sign that read THE LESBIAN AND GAY COMMUNITY SERVICES CENTER. I recognized the building; it was in the West Village, not far from our apartment.

I got up and moved closer to the TV as Bill Beutel's face returned to the screen.

"A Manhattan-based AIDS advocacy group that was formed just last week has expressed their relief at the drug's approval, but many still say that it's too little, too late."

A blond man in the crowd began to speak. The banner on the screen read *Joseph Taylor, AIDS Activist*. "While we're pleased that there is now a legal option that might be viable for some people who are dying of

AIDS, it's simply not enough," he said curtly. "AZT has been available to us on the black market for ages, and it's well known that it is too toxic for the majority of HIV and AIDS patients. For those who *are* able to tolerate it, it is a short-term solution that costs up to ten thousand dollars per year and is often not covered by insurance. Is the drug's approval a good thing? Yes. Is it enough? No. Are we going to continue to demand more from the government and pharmaceutical companies? We are. In fact, we're just getting started."

Bill Beutel's face reappeared next to a photograph of a man with brown hair wearing a lab coat. He went on. "Dr. Anthony Fauci, who is in his third year as the director of the National Institute of Allergy and Infectious Diseases, says that he understands the frustration of the AIDS activists and states that the drug was approved without traditional, rigorous trials because of the importance of prolonging the lives of those afflicted with HIV and AIDS. Meanwhile, Mayor Ed Koch was not available for comment. More after this." A commercial for Pop-Tarts appeared on the screen, and I remembered where I was. My heart thudded in frantic excitement. Was this it? Was this the cure we'd been waiting for?

Chapter Three

Filled with hope, I turned around, only to find Mom, Bob, and J.R. looking at me with the world's saddest eyes.

For a long moment, it was quiet. "Sarah?" Bob finally asked, kicking off one of those annoying coded conversations that adults like to have in front of kids. J.R. nodded in agreement that they should let me in on whatever it was that they were communicating silently about, and the momentary warmth I'd felt turned to dread.

I looked to Dad, wondering if he was going to weigh in on the mysterious and disappointing news that Mom,

Bob, and J.R. were about to share with me, but his eyes were closed, the oxygen mask fogging in slow pulses as he breathed.

"All right," Mom said, searching Bob's and then J.R.'s eyes one last time. "Sit back down, Iris. We'll fill you in."

Feeling numb, I sat carefully next to Dad's feet. He stirred. "How are you doing, Earthworm?" he whispered.

Had he heard the news broadcast? The conversation among Mom, Bob, and J.R.? Did he know about AZT? "Don't get excited," he whispered.

That answered my questions.

I imagined my heart in my hands, a cold, transparent, empty glass orb. Through it, my fingers looked distorted. "Dad's right," Mom said, taking my hand in hers. The imaginary paperweight clattered to the carpet. "It's nothing to get excited about. Not in terms of Dad, at least. We've already tried him on AZT."

"What?" I asked, tears stinging my eyes. "How is that possible? It said on the news that the drug was only approved today."

J.R. cleared his throat as if searching for words; I

could tell he was thinking about how to explain things in a way I could understand.

"I'm not a baby," I reminded him harshly.

"Very true," he agreed. "So here's the thing: For quite a while, medicines that might help treat HIV and AIDS have been circulating on the black market." He interrupted himself. "You know what I mean by the 'black market'?"

"Yes," I lied defensively, imagining a dark underground cave lined with pharmacies, all painted black. In my mind, black curtains hung in their darkened windows.

"Good. Yeah, so lots of people with HIV and AIDS have been trying out these drugs, experimenting with them, and talking to one another about which seem to help and which don't. Things are moving too slowly in the medical world in terms of coming up with treatments, so we—the people who are sick—have had to take matters into our own hands. Several months ago, when his symptoms started getting bad, your dad tried AZT. *Before* it was approved."

I glanced at Mom and Bob to see what they thought of all of this. Taking a drug before it was legal to do so? It definitely didn't seem like something that doctors would be in favor of.

Mom read my mind. "We thought it was worth it." *Because Dad was dying anyway.* She didn't have to say it out loud for me to understand.

"AZT is a drug that was created a while back to fight cancer," Bob said, leaning in and shifting into professor mode. This was something Bob did a lot. He didn't have kids of his own, which, I assumed, was why he sometimes talked to me like I was four and other times like I was fifty. Teacher-Bob might have been annoying, but because Bob was Bob, I didn't mind. "It didn't work for cancer, but it seems like it might help prolong the lives of some people with HIV and AIDS. *Might* and *some* being the operative words." He was starting to lose me, as he often did. Usually I didn't care, but this time I needed to understand what he was saying. He continued, "The scientific studies on AZT haven't been very scientific, but sometimes, you have to weigh the value of a human life against an unknown."

I looked to Mom, hoping she'd clarify.

"AZT might give some people who are HIV positive or have AIDS more time, but it's extremely harsh. It destroys your bone marrow. Dad couldn't tolerate it," she said.

"And he tried it even though it was illegal?" I asked, looking back to Bob, who had a really important job at the hospital and didn't seem like the kind of person who would be in favor of giving anyone illegal drugs.

Mom nodded.

"Could he try it again?" I asked, getting back to her comment about how Dad couldn't tolerate it. "Maybe it would work if he tried it again?"

"Remember about a month ago when Dad was in the hospital for a while?" Mom asked.

Of course I remembered. On Valentine's Day, Dad had gotten so tired that he couldn't move. His thin skin was as white as his sheets. Bob had come with a wheelchair, and J.R. had driven Dad off to one of the few hospitals that was even admitting HIV and AIDS patients. It was a terrible, depressing place, which was why, after he got better—well, *somewhat* better—Mom and Bob had set him up at home with a hospital bed and oxygen tank. *No way is he going back to that hellhole*, Mom had said. *No matter what.*

"He was at the hospital to get blood transfusions because the AZT made him severely anemic," Mom explained. Then, unlike Bob, she translated: "His red blood cells were shot. There's no point in trying AZT again. It would kill him."

"Mom's right," Dad rasped, and I turned around and looked at him—his skeletal face and clawlike hands.

He didn't look like Dad anymore. I hadn't realized he'd been listening so alertly. He went on, his voice thick and gurgling. "Once the transfusions were done, we got the hell out of that hellhole. Are there any other places where we can get *hell* into that sentence?" he asked.

I laughed through tears I hadn't realized were there. Mom, Bob, J.R., and Dad laughed, too, until Dad began coughing. And coughing and coughing and coughing.

———

"Roll, baby, roll, baby, roll, roll, ROLL!" Toby yelled as Julian jiggled the die in his hands. Mr. Inglash peeked over my shoulder at our makeshift game board on the way to his desk. Sometimes I got the sense that he was hoping we'd invite him to play with us, which, honestly, wouldn't have been so bad. He'd probably make a decent Dungeon Master.

"Seventeen," Julian announced after dumping the royal-blue die onto the table.

"Climb the mountain," Will said, pulling a baggie of pretzels and his slingshot out of his backpack. Then, sensing that we were waiting for more, he added, "There's, like, a goblin chasing you."

"That's it?" I asked. "Just 'a goblin'? I swear to God,

you are the worst Dungeon Master to ever play the game." I jumped out of my seat, and Toby and Will laughed as I ran to the window because they knew exactly what I was up to. I cranked it open, the rain that had nearly melted yesterday's dirty snow blowing onto my face. "Mallory!" I screamed in the direction of the empty playground. "Come back!"

Julian, Will, and Toby laughed, and Mr. Inglash smiled at us as I sat back down. Will crunched on a pretzel while loading another into his slingshot. He was such a weirdo. "Go long," he told Toby, who scooted his chair backward toward the wall.

"You'll shoot your eye out," I said, quoting *A Christmas Story.*

"This is a *catapult,* not a Red Ryder BB gun," Will reminded me. "Besides, it would be worth shooting my eye out to finally get a hole in one." He released the pretzel toward Toby's open mouth. It flew over his head, bounced off the wall, and fell into the garbage can.

"Three pointer!" Will yelled.

"What do you call a combination of riflery, golf, and basketball?" Toby asked. "Because that's what this sport should be named."

"Grifleball?" I asked.

"Griflepretzel?" Will suggested.

Mr. Inglash chuckled a little and then continued to pretend to ignore us as he graded papers. Julian smiled a bit, his braces glinting in the overhead lights. I listened to the rain and wondered whether Dad was listening to it, too. The clock on the wall ticked in time with the raindrops. Next to it, Nancy Reagan's face smiled down from the JUST SAY NO! poster that hung in most of the classrooms. What would the First Lady think if she knew that Dad had taken AZT illegally last month? Did saying yes to black-market AZT count as saying yes to drugs?

Will launched another pretzel at Toby, and the die sat untouched, the seventeen from Julian's roll still facing upward. "You good with a slingshot?" I asked Julian, making conversation.

"I don't know," he said.

"Want to try?"

"Yeah, sure," he answered.

"Will, pass your *catapult* over here? Julian wants to try it out, and then he's going to need it with him when he climbs the mountain," I joked, knowing that DnD was likely over for the day, if not the year. There was no point without Mallory.

"I want you to know that it took me forever to find

the perfect Y-shaped branch from which to create this weapon," Will told me. "It is mine and mine alone." He grinned and wiggled his eyebrows in my direction, taunting me.

I took the bait.

"You loser," I said, laughing as I jumped up and grabbed at it. Will hopped onto his chair and dangled the slingshot over my head. I swiped at it giddily. Just as I closed my hand around the branch, Will pulled it away. "Psych!" he yelled.

"Ouch!" I couldn't stop laughing. "You gave me a splinter!" My pointer finger was pierced with a minuscule shard of wood, and I held it up in the air. "I'm going to sue you for this, Will!"

Without warning, Mr. Inglash appeared beside us. "What's going on?" he asked nervously. His face looked pale, and I felt sorry for him because he was clearly so confused about what had happened. Did he not understand that we were joking? I looked around at Will, Toby, and Julian to make sure that none of them was lying on the floor in a pool of blood; Mr. Inglash seemed to think something really serious had happened. His glasses were sliding down his nose, as usual, but he didn't bother to push them back up.

"We're fine," Will said from where he stood on the chair, looking from me to Toby to Julian, mystified.

"Everything's good," I assured Mr. Inglash, squeezing my pointer finger while pressing on the sliver of wood with my nail, trying to dislodge it. A pinprick of blood appeared.

Mr. Inglash shoved his hands into his pants pockets, and then took them back out. "Let's get you to the nurse's office, Iris," he said. I squinted up at him, thinking he must be kidding. "And that slingshot, Will? Hand it here."

Will searched my eyes as if to ask what on earth was going on. Apprehensively, he held the slingshot in Mr. Inglash's direction. Mr. Inglash reached for the rubber band, not the wood, and, holding it away from his body, led me by the shoulder to the doorway. I looked back at Will, Toby, and Julian and shrugged as Mr. Inglash guided me into the hall.

I searched his face as we walked side by side toward Nurse Joan's office. When we rounded the corner by the front entranceway, his left hand tightened on my shoulder as if he was worried that I might try to run away. With his right hand, he continued to hold Will's slingshot at a distance. Confused, I looked down and watched our feet as they stepped side by side in unison, Mr. Inglash's brown leather shoes beside my pink ones. I looked at my fingertip where the tiny pinprick of blood had dried atop the splinter, and suddenly, in a warm rush, everything connected.

He knew.

I stumbled, and Mr. Inglash glanced at me from the corner of his eye. *Mr. Inglash knew.* He knew about Dad. Maybe he knew about all of it—the AIDS *and* the dying, and he thought that I might have it, too. That maybe I'd caught it from Dad, and that I'd been bleeding and I'd touched the slingshot and I was going to infect everyone—my friends, him.

My face burned. I felt suddenly nauseous, and it wasn't because I'd been awake from three to five a.m. again. If this were Ms. Staffio leading me down the hallway, terrified of me, of what might be inside me, rushing through my veins, it would be different. It would be better, because it would be expected. But this was *Mr. Inglash*, the best and weirdest teacher in the entire school, and he was scared of me because my dad had AIDS. He thought I might kill him.

I tried to take a step away from him, but he tightened his grip on my shoulder.

A few doors down from the nurse's office, our eyes met, and for just a moment, he seemed able to see everything I was thinking. He seemed able to feel what I was feeling. But then he gave my shoulder a little tap, pretended to smile, and guided me to the closed door of Nurse Joan's office.

Her office door was locked because it was already almost four o'clock. While Mr. Inglash fumbled with his keys, I silently begged my pulse to stop stamping against my eardrums. I felt too hot and wobbly, and to calm myself, I read the Shel Silverstein poem that someone had written in neat cursive on the outside of the green door. It was about little Peggy Ann McKay, who was playing sick to get out of going to school. "*I have the measles and the mumps, / a gash, a rash, and purple bumps,*" she complained. I thought about the measles. The mumps. The Black Plague. Yellow fever. All the illnesses that had terrified and killed people throughout time. And I thought about how now, all these other illnesses seemed so different from AIDS because people had learned about them— how to treat them, how to prevent them. Meanwhile, Mr. Inglash, who was so smart and kind, thought he was going to get AIDS from a splinter in a healthy person's finger. My healthy blood raced in fury through my healthy veins.

By the time Mr. Inglash got the door open and flicked on the lights, I was fuming. Who was this man? I had thought I knew him. He was calm and funny and never too serious. I searched his eyes through the thick lenses that he had yet to push up onto his nose, probably because he didn't want to touch his face after touching the shoulder that touched the arm that touched the hand that touched the finger that had a pinprick of dried blood on it, and *I didn't even have AIDS!*

I expected to see cruelty in his eyes, but instead I saw fear, and his fear made me even angrier. It made me mean. In the snottiest tone I could muster, I told him, "Your glasses are falling off again." I pushed away the threat of tears, feeling meaner than I'd ever felt before. "You can't get it through casual contact. Don't you know anything? Besides, I. Don't. Have. It." I drew out each word slowly and deliberately, all the while wondering: Would Dad be mad at me for how I was acting? Would he be strong enough when I saw him today to listen to the story? If he was, should I tell him? How much time was I wasting with Mr. Inglash *right now*, since Dad might be awake? And could things ever go back to normal at school after this?

Mr. Inglash removed his hand from my shoulder.

43

For a moment, I thought he might actually push his glasses back up onto his nose, but he didn't. He couldn't bring himself to. "I know," he said, dropping Will's slingshot into the garbage can. It landed atop a pile of used tissues. "I know all of that. Better safe than sorry, though," he added quietly. "There's still so much we don't know."

In that moment, I felt a hatred bigger and hotter than anything I'd felt before. If Mr. Inglash could be this scared of me, a healthy person whose dad had AIDS, how would the rest of the world treat me if they found out? *They'll treat her like a leper,* Dad had said. He'd been right. Of course, he'd been right.

Mr. Inglash rummaged through the nurse's supplies until he found a pair of rubber gloves in a dusty plastic bag at the bottom of a drawer. Pulling them on, he turned the sink faucet to *hot* and instructed me to wash my hands with soap. Steam rose as the water burned my hands, but the hot water must have removed the splinter because my fingertip no longer hurt when I pressed on it. I wanted to cry, but I wouldn't give Mr. Inglash that satisfaction.

After a while, he handed me some paper towels and, with still-gloved hands, wrapped two Band-Aids around my finger. The tiny mark was so invisible that he'd wrapped them too low, but I didn't say anything. I knew it didn't matter.

Back in the classroom, Will and Toby were laughing about something, and Julian was sitting on the low counter next to the fish tank. "Where's my catapult?" Will asked, grinning, when I stormed through the doorway.

"Ask Mr. Inglash," I said, ripping off the Band-Aids and throwing them away.

"Where'd he go?" Toby asked, poking his head out the classroom door.

I shrugged. "Maybe he's still in the nurse's office? I don't know."

Toby scrunched his nose like he wanted to ask me what had happened but was also scared to. That was fine with me; there was no way I could tell them what was wrong without letting them know that Dad had AIDS, that Dad was dying of AIDS, that Dad was *dying*. Everything that was happening was too much, and as I grabbed my backpack and yanked the zipper shut, I wondered: If Mallory were still here, would I finally be able to bring myself to tell her? When I forced myself to think rationally about it, I knew that she wouldn't judge me *or* Dad. Suddenly, I missed her more than I had since the snowy morning three months ago when Will, Toby, and I had stood outside her Union Square apartment waving goodbye as her family drove off in their brown station wagon.

I was glad when Will changed the subject. "I guess we should go home early?" he half asked, half stated, shoving his empty pretzel baggie into his pocket and pulling his sweatshirt on.

Toby and Julian grabbed their jackets.

"Hey, Julian, where do you live, anyway?" Toby asked as we headed toward the front doors. He was trying to make things feel fine and normal, which was something that I typically liked about Toby, but today it annoyed me.

"Union Square," Julian responded.

"That's not far from Iris's apartment," Will told him.

I didn't think that I could tell Dad what had happened, but I wondered if I should tell Mom. Then I wondered how Mr. Inglash had found out about Dad in the first place.

"Julian lives right by where Mallory lived," Will went on, nudging me. "You guys are sort of neighbors."

"What's your point, Will?" I asked, pushing through

the front doors of the building and pulling up my hood against the drizzle. I felt bad about being so mean to my friends, but I couldn't stop myself.

"No point," Will said. "Jeez. Just that you can walk partway home together, that's all." I rolled my eyes at him, at everything that he didn't know and would never be able to understand, as he and Toby exchanged a look before saying goodbye.

"Let's go," I said brusquely to Julian, guiding him toward Park Avenue. We dodged people with umbrellas and a soaking-wet kid on a bike. I sneaked a glance at him from the corner of my eye as we crossed Twentieth. He was watching me but looked down when our eyes connected. I was still fuming, but I had to admit to myself that I was also glad for the company. I didn't feel like being alone.

Chapter Four

The rain picked up, and Julian and I tugged at the drawstrings on our hoods as we made our way south. I didn't know what to say to him; I had so many thoughts about Mr. Inglash swirling through my mind.

And Julian wasn't exactly the world's greatest conversationalist. In fact, he was the polar opposite of Mallory, who I'd walked home with every day from the time we'd become friends until she'd moved. She was funny and smart and never stopped talking, which I guess some people found annoying, but it never bothered me. I stepped around a puddle. Julian's silence made me miss her even more; I needed a distraction.

Thunder rumbled. On the corner of Seventeenth Street, we passed a kid in a raincoat pushing an old man in a wheelchair, and an image of Dad at home in his hospital bed barged into my mind with such force that I nearly gasped. Dad's body was shrinking so quickly. Fading so fast. I wondered how many weeks or months it would be until I'd be walking down this same street and no longer have a father. Tears threatened to burst from my eyes. And Mr. Inglash. Mr. Inglash didn't care about any of that; he cared only about himself. His own stupid, irrational fear.

The light at the corner changed, and Julian and I began crossing with a crowd of people. I couldn't stop thinking about Mr. Inglash and how wrong he was. About everything. There wasn't even a mark on my finger anymore. Not even a tiny, pale line. I stopped walking and held my finger in front of my face, not caring how weird I might look to anyone else. My finger was *fine*. It was *completely fine*. And even if it weren't fine, I didn't have AIDS. But that didn't feel like the point either, because if I did have AIDS, nobody would have caught it because I got a splinter. And either way, if somebody did have AIDS, they shouldn't be treated like it was their *fault*. Then I thought of J.R. and Dad.

I supposed *fault* did play a role.... But that barely felt like the right word, and besides, would that make it less terrible to be sick with a deadly mystery illness? I didn't know. I didn't know anything anymore.

"Iris?" Julian called from the corner. I looked up from my finger and realized I was alone in the middle of the street, crying. "What are you doing?" He glanced anxiously at the stoplight as it turned green. "Cars are coming!" A few passersby stared from Julian to me, but Julian didn't seem to care about how weird they probably thought we both were.

A cabbie stuck his head out the window into the rain and yelled at me to move it, so I forced my legs to work and ran to the sidewalk just as the cab sped past me, splashing through a puddle. Muddy water soaked my pants.

"What...I mean, why..." Julian stopped trying to speak and stared at me. He probably wanted to yell at me. Or maybe he wanted to know why I had been standing there like that, staring at my finger in the intersection. He seemed stuck between silence and words, just like I was stuck in my thoughts about Dad and Mr. Inglash. Between wanting to tell someone and wanting to hide.

Wiping my eyes with my rain-soaked sleeves, I

wondered, if Mallory were here, would this be the moment that I'd finally tell her that Dad was dying of AIDS?

I wiped my eyes again, looked down at my mud-soaked shoes and then back to Julian. He appeared unfazed that the people passing us were staring, which made him feel relatable somehow. My body was swollen with feelings. Now that Mr. Inglash knew about Dad and was terrified of me, everything seemed like too much to keep to myself. I flinched as my emotions boiled, burning me. "My dad is dying of AIDS," I blurted out.

"What?" Julian asked, his face falling, because what else is there to say when someone tells you a thing like that? But it felt good to say it aloud.

"You're the only one who knows. I mean, you're the only one I've told. Somehow Mr. Inglash knows, which is why he totally panicked when I got a splinter. Because of, you know, the blood. And if he knows, all the teachers probably know, and what my dad said would happen is coming true: Everyone's going to treat me like a total outcast." I was crying again. Julian stared at me like he didn't know what to say. But at the same time, I couldn't help noticing that he didn't seem scared to be standing close to me. He seemed . . . sad for me.

That's awful, I pictured him saying. *I'm so sorry.*

"Do you know that people call AIDS the 'gay plague'?" I went on.

"Is your dad gay?" he asked, tilting his head to the side.

"Yes," I responded, immediately defensive. "Do you care?"

"No. I mean, I *care*, but not in a bad way. One of my mom's best friends is gay. We haven't seen him in forever, because he lives in Colorado."

I nodded, finally taking a breath. I didn't expect him to continue speaking, but he went on. "Remember how I told you I'm from Indiana?" he asked. "Well, *most recently*, anyway. We move constantly. But that's another story. We lived one town over from Ryan White. You've heard of him, right?"

"Yeah," I said. Of course I'd heard of Ryan White. Everyone had. A couple of years back he'd gotten HIV through a blood transfusion, and his school had banned him from attending because they were scared that he was going to pass it to other people.

Julian pushed his wet curls to the side of his forehead. "So I know some stuff about AIDS," he concluded.

"That's the most you've ever said," I pointed out,

surprised out of my tears. I wiped my cheeks. "You don't really talk much."

What's your name again? Mrs. Obvious? I envisioned him asking, and I almost smiled at what my imagined version of him had said.

"I know. When your family moves as much as mine, it kind of messes with you. And I'm sorry. About your dad."

I nodded in thanks, wondering what was up with his family but not wanting to pry. Julian felt both familiar and unfamiliar, like he understood maybe the tiniest thing about what I was going through while, at the same time, still being a total stranger. I imagined a paperweight heart beating in his chest and, despite my fiery swirl of emotions, I wanted to see it better.

"I'd better go," he said, before I could figure out what to say next. "My mom will be worried if I get home late. We've only lived in small towns before, and she keeps reminding me to be careful because I'm a country mouse in the big city."

I laughed, imagining whiskers sprouting on his cheeks, and we said goodbye. For a while, I stood in the rain watching him walk down Seventeenth Street, past Union Square Park. Despite my clutter of feelings about Mr. Inglash and Dad, I wondered why Julian's family moved around so much. How long would he be in Manhattan for? Even though I'd just met him, already I was dreading the day that he'd leave.

———————

MORE *by Steven Cohen*
March 20, 1987

Mesmerize me: ancient stains on wallpaper, toast
    crumbs
On newspaper, outside,
Raindrops against glass (each a world) I want
Everything, more and more and more.

In my bedroom, I emptied the drenched contents of my backpack onto the rug and arranged my books and papers alongside the radiator. Then I changed clothes and snapped Dad's barely legible poem into the binder. I tried to not focus on the deterioration of his handwriting or how his lettering had become so light that it was almost gone.

Upstairs, I sat next to him while J.R. took a shower. Dad was on his side, knees pulled up toward his chest like the fetuses in Mom's medical books. I'd never seen him in that position before, and it scared me because it made him seem sicker. There was plenty of room next to him on his bed; he appeared even thinner than he had yesterday, his rib cage protruding beneath his gray sweatshirt. How could someone so thin still be alive?

I ran my finger where the splinter had been, across his bony fingers and to the edge of the purple sarcoma on the back of his hand. It wasn't an open wound, but I couldn't bring myself to touch it. My eyes burned with tears again. Maybe I was just like Mr. Inglash.

Identify the beating heart of what's important. Then write around it.

I sat next to Dad, opened a notebook that was on the side table, and wrote *SHAME* along the side of the page.

SHAME *by Iris Cohen*
March 20, 1987

Show me that splinter in your finger, but not so I can
Help you. I
Am scared of you. I'm scared of your blood. You
    trusted
Me but now MY fear is
Everything.

Then I ripped out the page, crumpled it into a tight ball, and threw it into the garbage can. I curled up beside Dad and shut my eyes.

But this time, I didn't sleep. Dad's breathing felt different. Worse. Like more of a struggle. It would be dinnertime soon, but it didn't seem like J.R. had started cooking anything. When he got out of the shower, he sat down in a chair on the other side of Dad, his hair still wet and dripping slightly onto his light blue shirt. He held Dad's hand and looked out the window.

I didn't feel like myself. The world didn't feel like the world. Was this real? I wished J.R. would leave. I wished he would go off somewhere and never come back. I turned over so I wouldn't have to look at him, and my back touched Dad's back. His spine. From above, did we look like two fetuses? One healthy and one sick?

How did I end up with two poets for roommates? Mom used to joke. *How am I the only scientist here? You guys are two peas in a pod.*

It wasn't even five o'clock, but Bob and Mom tapped on the door and let themselves in. Mom pulled in a portable IV stand that she must have taken from the hospital, and Bob placed a brown paper lunch bag on the kitchen counter next to the coffee maker. After washing up, Mom and J.R. rolled Dad onto his back. I couldn't tell if he was awake or asleep. I got up and watched her put on rubber gloves before pulling up his loose sweatshirt sleeve. I looked away as she inserted a needle into his vein.

"Why does Dad need that?" I asked, my eyes blurred with tears. I didn't want to see a needle go into Dad's arm. I didn't want to see his blood; I didn't want to see *anyone's* blood.

"It's just pain medicine," Mom said quietly.

I turned back around. "Are you in pain?" I asked Dad.

He didn't respond, and his chest rattled as he breathed. How long could he go on like this? "How long *exactly...*," I started to ask as I sat back down next to Dad, but I stopped myself. I couldn't ask the question.

Mom pulled off the rubber gloves and put them into a special wastebasket that she and Bob used for medical stuff. I wasn't allowed anywhere near it. Then she washed up, sat carefully next to me on Dad's bed, and rested her head on the top of mine.

"Not long," she answered in a whisper.

Weeks? By April? When would I wake up and be fatherless?

"How was school?" she asked absently, as if on autopilot.

I thought again of Mr. Inglash. "Fine," I told her. I couldn't be like him, so I kissed Mom on the cheek and lay back down, resting my head next to Dad's again. I wrapped my arm around him, taking special care to touch the bandages Mom had placed over the IV needle.

Bob offered to run out and pick up something for dinner. J.R. suggested Dad's favorite Mediterranean place on Broadway. Mom went downstairs to change, while J.R. turned on the news and began clearing off the kitchen table. Dad squeezed my hand.

I tried to remember how he used to look. Before. Before he had gotten sick. Before the divorce. Before J.R. Before all of this. Weakly, he reached for his oxygen mask. I knew he wanted to say something—he hated talking with it on—so I pulled it away from his face for him.

"Earthworm," he whispered, his eyes still closed. "Promise me you'll always be a poet." The breath inside him sounded as if it were wheezing through each individual hole in a strainer.

"Okay," I told him, trying not to cry. That was a promise I knew I could keep.

"And give J.R. a chance." Each word was so quiet. Such a struggle. "He wants to know you. I want him to know you."

"I'm not mean to him."

"Stubborn girl." He smiled a little. It looked like it hurt him to do it, and I laid my head on his bony chest, careful not to crush him. He seemed so fragile. How did he become so breakable? "You know what I mean."

"Say yes to him?"

"Say yes to everything."

"Everything?" I pictured the poster of Nancy Reagan hanging in the classroom.

Dad laughed a tiny bit and then coughed. "Almost everything," he mumbled. I could tell he was still smiling.

That night, I fell asleep next to him in his bed. Outside the window, cars honked, and every now and then sirens wailed. At some point, I opened my eyes and found myself in Bob's arms in the brightly lit elevator, and then someone was pulling my covers to my chin. On Saturday morning, I stumbled out of bed to the front door for my poem. My pink Converse and some flecks of mud rested on the doormat, but nothing else.

Dad was gone.

Chapter Five

SPLITTING *by Steven Cohen*

September 22, 1985

Slowly (almost) unnoticed the

Peony thickened, stalks multiplying invisibly

Like cells (life, growing) before our eyes until

It was enormous. Stems fumbled for

Thin fragments of sun.

They were crowding themselves out.

I was just a kid. Sunshine shone through thick air.

Now is the time, my dad told me. It's going to die.

Go get the shovel. Split it in half.

It was the third poem in the navy binder, after "ACROS-TIC" and Dad's second poem, "SORRY," and I stared at it for a long time as I sat at my desk, reading it with my eyes but not my brain. Almost two days had passed since Dad died. I had the red binder now, too, from upstairs—the one with my poems to Dad in it; J.R. had brought it down yesterday. There was a bluish-purple smudge of something on Dad's poem next to the *G* in *Go*. When the smudge was made, Dad had been alive. He'd been alive, and maybe he'd made it with a leaky pen or a drip of grape juice, and now I'd never know. I'd never know the millions and millions of things that Dad had never told me or taught me, because now he was dead. *Dad was dead. Dad was dead.*

Dad was dead.

The thought made me furious, and the rage felt like acid in my stomach. But then, just like that, the anger bubbled up, evaporating, and I was left with insides as enormous and open as the universe.

In the kitchen, the TV was on. The rhythm of a newscaster's deep voice forced its way under my closed door, but I couldn't make out what he was saying.

Outside the window, a helicopter hummed. The radiator sputtered.

After Mom and Dad had gotten divorced, but before we'd learned that Dad was HIV positive, he and I had gone to an exhibit on gravity at the American Museum of Natural History. A display on the wall described what would happen if Earth's gravitational pull suddenly switched off. It explained how lighter objects would float off to space first, followed by heavier objects, and how eventually Earth would break into chunks and float away, too. Everyone and everything would die.

I had broken into chunks. I was floating into space.

Was this how it felt to be dead?

A knock at my bedroom door startled me. "Honey?" Mom asked, and then, without waiting for my response, she gently pushed open the door. Her hair was a mess. Dark bags sagged beneath her eyes. "Can I join you?"

I nodded, and she lay down on my unmade bed. Then she looked from me to the ceiling and back to me again as if she didn't know what to say or do. It was just after six o'clock, and I hadn't left my room all day, aside from going to the bathroom. It was so much harder to do things when gravity was trying to suck you out to space.

I could tell that Mom understood. She patted the rumpled sheets next to her, and I lay by her side.

My bedroom faced east, so it never got much sun late in the day. "It's getting dark," I told Mom. My throat felt weird when I spoke, maybe because those were the first words I'd said since yesterday.

"Yeah," she agreed, and even though she was a scientist, not a poet like me and Dad, I knew she understood that I was speaking figuratively. Then, for a long time, we were both quiet. I closed my eyes because lying next to Mom helped restore the gravitational pull. At first, it was a relief to feel myself coming back together, but then, as my pieces fused, acidic anger flooded my stomach once again. It clawed at my insides, a bug-thick ocean.

I sat up quickly; the sudden anger made me want to move, and I could tell that Mom was trying to figure out what might be going through my head. *There's a deep, deep ocean in that mind of yours*, she used to say when she couldn't figure out what I was thinking about. She was right.

"You know, you haven't eaten," Mom said, motioning to the old grilled cheese and lukewarm glass of water that had been sitting on my desk for hours. I'd seen them, but my fragmenting mind hadn't registered their purpose. "J.R. called," she went on. "He's bringing down a casserole that one of his and Dad's friends dropped off. And Bob will be here soon."

I nodded, not knowing why we needed Bob anymore now that Dad was dead. *Dad was dead.*

Dad was dead.

The bugs in my stomach rushed together, creating one organism that instantly swamped my veins and set my blood on fire. I couldn't sit still. "Why is Dad dead?" I asked. I hadn't meant to say it aloud, and the anger in my voice frightened me.

"Oh, honey," Mom said, tears running down her cheeks, and in that strange moment of dim light and disassembling pieces of myself, I couldn't figure out why she was crying rather than helping me destroy something. I got up and paced around my room a bit. I could have run a mile. A marathon. I wanted to break something. Something important and delicate.

The doorbell rang. "Let's go try to eat some dinner," Mom suggested, wiping her eyes. "Maybe it will make us feel better."

I didn't want to feel better, but I let Mom hug me. Then, gently, mindlessly, she rested her hand on my shoulder to guide me to the bedroom door. Her touch jolted me, and an image of the school hallway between Mr. Inglash's classroom and the nurse's office unfolded in my mind like a storyboard. I remembered Mr. Inglash at my side. The splinter, the scalding water, the shame, and I jerked my body away from Mom's hand. Startled, she looked at me like she didn't know who I was. Then she went to answer the door.

For a few minutes, I stood in my bedroom feeling the tug of gravity. The scorching flames in my veins. Without really listening, I heard Mom thank Bob for bringing flowers. "Tulips! My favorite," she said. I heard J.R. caution Mom to be careful with the hot casserole dish. And finally, to prevent myself from floating away entirely, I went to the dining room to join them.

"Hey, Ear-ris," Bob joked when he saw me, but in a sad kind of way.

"How's it going, kid?" J.R. asked. He sounded exhausted and looked more in line with how I felt, his jaw clenched like he was trying to crush a marble between his teeth. And even though I found comfort in the familiarity of that look, I wanted to shove the steaming casserole dish off the table, onto his legs and feet. I pictured the dish shattering, scalding noodles burning him through his jeans, and I liked the thought of it. He *should* feel pain. He *deserved* to feel pain.

Our eyes met. As usual, I was pretty sure he could read my mind. And as I looked at him—his gray curls; faded, too-loose jeans; oversize sweatshirt; and eyes like deep, deep water—I felt the distinct sensation that my bug-infested rage monster was part of a larger organism and that that larger organism was also inhabiting him. Was his rage making him mean, too? If so, how was he hiding it?

Oblivious to my thoughts of shattered casserole dishes and bug-ridden darkness, Bob carried the vase of tulips to the table, and Mom took out four paper plates. J.R. went to the kitchen sink to fill the water pitcher. The bugs came together again into one being that slithered from my stomach and into my brain, where it pounded on my eyes and ears from within. How were Mom, J.R., and Bob getting dinner ready as if Dad hadn't just *died*? What was wrong with them?

"Mom!" I yelled. Startled, the three of them turned to me.

"What is it, honey?" Mom asked, a hint of frustration in her voice.

I didn't know what to say. What was happening? Was this real life? "Why didn't you tell me?" I screamed at her. "Why didn't you tell me that he was going to die *so soon?*"

J.R. turned off the faucet but stood still at the sink. Bob looked down at the floor. And Mom's entire body shrank like she was folding in on herself. Like she was dying, too.

I ran to my bedroom and slammed the door as hard as I could. The sound echoed off my walls, shaking my furniture. A picture frame on my desk fell face-forward, and I heard the sound of breaking glass. Crashing the door shut like that had felt good, so I slammed it again and again, envisioning spiderweb cracks on the windows splintering deeper and deeper with each bang, until finally I felt better.

Chapter Six

I sat at my desk, armpits prickling with sweat. Breathing heavily, I flipped through Dad's poems until I got to the one I was looking for.

FIRST *by Steven Cohen*
September 29, 1985

Find me at Audrey's party? she asked, eyes twinkling.

    Of course,

I said yes. It was 1970. She was the first person I

Recognized myself in. She was my home. I

Said I'll love you forever. It was the

Truth.

I stayed in my room for what felt like forever until finally I heard J.R. and Bob leave. The whole apartment was dark, but I didn't bother to turn on any lights as I made my way to the kitchen. A plate of casserole awaited me in the fridge, and just as I put it into the microwave, Mom appeared in the doorway.

"Hey, hon," she said softly.

"Hi," I answered as she filled a glass of water at the sink and handed it to me. Then she rested her chin gently on the top of my head, and together in silence, we watched the microwave count down.

I thought about Dad's poem and how he had recognized himself in Mom. Even though the two of them were so different, I knew what he meant. They *felt* similar.

"You know what Dad would say right now," she said, and I could hear a little smile in her voice as we stood there in the light of the microwave and the darkness of the kitchen.

"Yeah," I replied, smiling, too.

When I'd told Dad that Mom was getting a microwave, he'd cut out several newspaper articles about the possibility of dangerous electromagnetic waves seeping through the seals of these new appliances. Mom had assured him that she'd researched everything and that microwaves were perfectly safe, but still, he'd warned us not to stand too close while it was on.

I smiled at the memory, wondering if I should write a poem entitled "MICROWAVE." But then I remembered that there would be nobody to give it to.

When I woke up the next morning, I was hungry again, which seemed selfish and wrong. It was Monday, but Mom and I had decided that we were both taking the week off. Since spring break was coming up, I wouldn't have to go back to school for three weeks. And while I was glad not to have to deal with anyone at school, especially Mr. Inglash, part of me wanted to see him. To scream at him until he cried and begged me for forgiveness.

I found Mom on the living room couch looking blankly out the window at the buildings across the street and, beyond them, the gray March sky. Her eyes were puffy, and she was wearing the same jeans and sweater she'd worn yesterday. When she patted the couch next to her, I sat, but staying still felt unsettling.

"I'm glad you slept. How are you doing?" she asked, hugging me.

"I don't know," I told her. "Antsy." *I want to run ten miles*, I imagined saying. *Twenty miles. I want to throw things at the windows that look out over the Village. I want to shatter everything; I want to shatter the entire world.* I pictured myself picking up the vase filled with Bob's tulips from the coffee table and slamming it against the floor. I could see the exploding glass and red petals, wilting in a puddle of water. I thought of hurling the world atlas from the bookshelf at the wall, its heavy corners tearing holes through paint and drywall. But then I imagined it falling onto Mom, hurting her, which made me think of all the things that had caused her pain. Like J.R. "Where's J.R.?" I asked.

"He's coming down soon with breakfast. Some of his and Dad's friends sent over a tray."

I nodded, then got up and looked out the windows, all the way down to the top of the green-and-white-striped awning that covered the front door of our building. The street was quiet, the small trees still mostly bare. I tapped my fingernails against the window frame and stared at the sidewalk until my eyes began to sting. Then I wandered into the kitchen and flipped on the TV.

J.R. let himself into the apartment just as the news came on. From the kitchen doorway, I watched him for a minute before he noticed me. He took his sneakers off while balancing a tray in one hand. His face, despite the exhaustion, looked soft. The thing about J.R. was that part of me truly did hate him. He hadn't known he was sick when he and Dad started dating, and he *still* didn't feel sick, but he'd given Dad HIV. He'd infected him. The fact that it had been an accident didn't make it go away.

But at the same time, everything about him felt quiet and gentle, like the whisperwarm. Once, after we'd reread the first Anastasia book, I'd asked Dad if that was why he loved him—because he was the whisperwarm— and Dad had said yes. *I never would have thought to put it into those words, but that's exactly why I love him*, he'd told me.

Since recognizing yesterday that J.R. and I seemed to be inhabited by the same rage monster, I'd felt better about focusing on the part of him that I didn't hate, on the whisperwarm.

He pushed his key into his back pocket, looked up, and saw me standing there. *Hey, Earthworm*, I imagined him saying but, of course, he didn't. "Hey, kid," he said instead. "We've got bagels."

I nodded and shoved my bangs out of my eyes. In the kitchen, Mom cleared the countertop near the stove for the tray. A yellow envelope rested on top of a poppy seed bagel, its corner smudged with cream cheese from one of the plastic containers. *To: J.R., Sarah, Iris, and Bob*, it read. I lifted the plastic wrap and pulled out the card as Mom turned up the news.

"Last night, Dr. Anthony Fauci responded to a growing number of AIDS activists by once again acknowledging their frustration. However, people with AIDS and their allies want more," the newscaster's voice said. The camera scanned a crowd of angry-looking people outside the Lesbian and Gay Community Services Center—the same one they'd shown on the news when I'd learned that AZT had been approved.

The channel-seven newscaster held a microphone to a young man with a light brown ponytail who was half talking, half shouting. "We are losing our community members left and right to this virus, and drug companies are silent. Politicians are silent. President Reagan will barely even utter the word *AIDS*!" He shook with anger.

"What about ribavirin?" another man yelled, pushing his way forward. "It's less toxic than AZT, and it's about to gain approval in Britain. The only place to get this possibly lifesaving treatment is through the black market in Mexico. We *demand* that the FDA approve it here. And not only ribavirin. We want Ampligen and we want Glucan. We want DTC and we want ddC. We want AS 101 and MTP-PE and AL 721. We want all the potentially lifesaving treatments that the FDA refuses to approve, because the people who are dying are being ignored. And why are so many of them being ignored? Why are so many of *us* being ignored?" He swept his arm in an arc, indicating the group of people next to him. *"Because we are gay."* Then he said it again. "We are dying because we are gay." My breath caught in my chest, and I swallowed hard as he went on. "That's one of the many reasons why we have come together as an advocacy group. Because we're going to fight this."

J.R. rubbed his hand through his hair as the scene shifted back to the newsroom and eventually to a traffic accident on the Long Island Expressway. Mom excused herself to go to her bedroom. I couldn't turn off the man's voice: *We are dying because we are gay.*

Was that true?

"So how are you holding up, kid?" J.R. asked, and I didn't know if his question was in reference to Dad dying or the newscast, or maybe both. Because maybe both were, at their core, the same thing. I searched his eyes and shrugged.

"Go ahead and open the card," he said as he went to the sink to wash his hands. "Read it to me."

Monday 3/23/87

Dearest J.R., Sarah, Iris, and Bob,
    Our deepest condolences. We loved Steven.
We'll continue to fight in his memory.
       With love,
       Your family of fellow activists

Our family of fellow activists? I looked at J.R. "Just like on the news," I said.

He smiled at me a little, his jaw still clenched. God, he looked exhausted. "Yeah, kid," he said. "The same exact group that was on the news."

After I hung the card on the fridge with a magnet, J.R. and I sat at the table with bagels and cream cheese on paper plates because apparently, when your dad dies, you eat off paper. J.R. smiled a tired smile and caught my eye. It was like looking in a mirror—we were both a combination of exhausted and furious, and this similarity between us made me think about one of Dad's poems. It was called "WATCHING." I closed my eyes and pictured it.

WATCHING *by Steven Cohen*
October 8, 1985

When you think

About the future spread before you, it's
    important

To remember that the measurement of time is a
    human

Creation. Time, itself, just is. Open the back of

His watch. Peek

Inside. See golden gears

Nudging golden gears? See tiny knobs locking

Gently into open spaces?

Even though I'd been starving just a few moments before, eating felt weird. J.R. must have been thinking the same thing, because he said, "I don't know how we can even eat," and I knew what he was saying: How could we eat when Dad was dead and gone and would never eat again?

The thought, like most of my thoughts, made me want to throw something. I eyed my untouched sesame seed bagel with veggie cream cheese, and I must have looked from it to the wall, because J.R. said, "It won't be satisfying. The bagel's too soft. Plus the cream cheese will just be a mess to clean up."

I couldn't help smiling as I took a bite.

"Your dad didn't tell you much about the advocacy work he'd been doing," J.R. went on matter-of-factly.

"No," I confirmed. I knew what advocacy was, and Dad had even written a poem by that title, but I didn't know what kind of work "advocacy work" was.

"Well, I'll tell you about it sometime," he said. "Your dad wanted me to." Then, seemingly out of nowhere, he picked up half of his poppy seed bagel and hurled it at the wall. For a second, the cream cheese glued it to the wallpaper before it slid to the floor.

I was so shocked that I burst into laughter. Then I threw mine against the wall, too, and soon we were both hysterical. He'd been right. It hadn't been very satisfying, and the cream cheese *was* really hard to get out of the rug.

But it made me feel a little bit better.

—————

Even though it was barely afternoon, the day felt a million years old. Mom was napping on the couch. Again. Her brown hair hung over her face, and she snored gently, the beige crocheted blanket rising and falling. "All this sadness is making me so tired," she'd explained, apologizing, before lying down.

Back when Dad had first moved in with J.R., she'd been the same way. Sad. Just so sad all the time. I flipped through the red binder until I found the poem that I'd written about it.

WINDOW *by Iris Cohen*
October 22, 1985

What was
I thinking? she sobbed quietly.
    How did I
Not see? I am so
Damn stupid. She walked

Over to the dark window and rested her head
    against the
Wide expanse of glass.

Then I found the poem in the navy binder by the
same title: Dad's response.

WINDOW *by Steven Cohen*
October 23, 1985

Watch carefully as
I open this miniature window into my mind. Climb
    in, but
Noiselessly. I'll show you the *why*.
Do you see that fireplace, never-been-used? Grandpa
    Fred? His whiskey
On the end table? Do you see Grandma Bea
    sweeping the clean
Wood beneath his feet?

Chapter Seven

It seemed to me that, in addition to eating off paper plates for every meal, when your dad dies, people come and go from your house all day long. Earlier, Bob and J.R. had hung around for a while, and as soon as they'd left, two of Mom's friends had shown up. When *they'd* left, Bob had returned with a pint of Mom's favorite rocky road ice cream. Now he was wiping down the countertops, and the doorbell rang again.

I hadn't thought much about Will, Toby, or even Julian, so when I opened the door to find the three of them standing there, I was kind of shocked. Under normal circumstances, Will and Toby would have shoved their way in and headed straight to the snack cabinet in the kitchen, but these weren't normal circumstances, so they stood in the doorway self-consciously until Julian gave them a little shove from behind, and they stumbled inside.

"Hi," I said. I'd never felt uncomfortable around Will or Toby, but suddenly, I didn't know what to do with my hands. I crossed my arms and then uncrossed them. The fact that they were here meant that they probably knew everything. I wondered if they'd call Mallory and tell her what had happened. I hoped they would. The thought of explaining everything felt impossible.

"Hey," Toby replied awkwardly, wiping his nose with the back of his hand. Will took his hand out of his jacket pocket, waved, and then shoved it back in. Julian smiled at me awkwardly like he didn't know what to do or say.

The last time I'd seen Will and Toby at school, the only thing they'd known was that Mom and Dad were divorced because Dad was gay. Whenever they'd come over, I'd been at Mom's apartment; I'd never brought them upstairs to Dad and J.R.'s. And now, here they were, visiting me because Dad had died of AIDS. Were they mad at me for keeping Dad's sickness from them?

Did they not understand how judgmental everyone was about AIDS? The very possibility that they'd be angry at me made *me* mad at *them*, even though they hadn't done anything. *Yet.* The tiny bugs were reawakening, morphing from individual organisms and gelling into a massive, flaming scorch mark.

"So you guys want to come in or what?" I asked, not waiting for their response. I led them to the dining table. There was a small blob of veggie cream cheese on one of the chairs that J.R. and I had missed when we'd cleaned up. I wiped it off with a napkin before sitting down.

"My mom made these," Julian said softly, pushing a paper plate of cookies covered in plastic wrap to the center of the table. "They're chocolate chip." When our eyes met, he smiled a little before looking away, like maybe he understood how breakable I felt. Toby and Will avoided eye contact with me.

How had they all found out? Who had told them? Who else knew? I felt too warm as heat crept up my scalp and the backs of my legs and was relieved when Bob joined us, a yellow dishrag thrown over his shoulder. "Not *more* food! I just finished cleaning up," he joked, pulling the plastic wrap off of the plate of cookies. "All right, go ahead. Make more crumbs."

Will and Toby exchanged a glance as if to ask each other, *Who is this guy?* and it hit me again how much they didn't know. How much Mallory didn't know. None of them had any idea that Bob had just magically popped onto the scene a few months ago to help us take care of Dad. And they certainly didn't know anything about J.R. They were my best friends, and they didn't even know me.

"I'm Bob," Bob said, waving to Will, who was on the far side of the table. Then he held out his hand to Toby, who was closest to him. "Nice to meet you," he said, and I cringed, imagining the boogers on Toby's hand that Bob was about to touch.

"You too," Toby said quietly. He shook Bob's hand and then looked down at his own as if to inspect it for germs. *Bob's germs.* "I'm Toby," he mumbled, still studying his palm. I felt my shoulders tighten and my jaw clench.

Unaware of how strangely Toby was acting, Bob held out his hand to Julian. "Hey, there," he said.

"Hey," Julian said, shaking Bob's hand. "I'm Julian." Then Julian took a cookie and offered the plate to Toby and then Will, both of whom passed. I looked from Toby's blue eyes to Will's brown ones. Neither of them had ever passed up food before. Never. And especially not cookies. They looked away from me.

"So we heard about your dad," Will finally said, still avoiding eye contact as Bob returned to the kitchen to get the milk.

"Yeah, we're sorry," Toby added. "We didn't know he was sick with...he had...you know." He looked down. He couldn't even say it. I shut my eyes in an attempt to contain the acid. The bug-comprised monster. Both were searching for outlets, threatening to spill over. If Dad had died of something other than AIDS— cancer, a heart attack, *anything*—their reactions would have been different. They'd be eating cookies and asking me how I was doing and what they could do to help. Chunks of me broke off from my arms, my stomach, the back of my head. I was floating out to space again.

In the kitchen, Bob opened the refrigerator with a snap of suction. He closed it. He shuffled through cabinets. Cardboard boxes brushed cardboard boxes. Then he flipped on the radio. The news was on.

"*Fifteen percent* of Americans still believe that people with HIV and AIDS should be tattooed as a means of identifying them, and many Americans are still talking about the benefits of quarantining those who are afflicted. NPR's medical correspondent is here to weigh in on whether these measures are necessary, or if we should trust people's self-reporting on the subject," a woman's voice said. Bob snapped the radio off. I looked down at my fingernails, trying to calm myself. Trying to gather my broken pieces. *She'll be a leper. She'll be a leper. She'll be a leper.*

"Hello?" J.R. called from the front hallway. "It's me. I have more food." Then to himself, "How much food do they think we can eat?" The familiarity of his voice stitched my pieces together, bringing me back to life.

"Hey, kid," J.R. said, coming into the dining room with a couple of envelopes in one hand and a pan of something that resembled lasagna in the other. "I didn't know you had company." He smiled at Toby, Will, and Julian in turn. "I'm J.R.," he told them. "You must be Iris's friends from school." Despite his obvious exhaustion, J.R. was friendly, as always. He pointed at Toby with the envelopes and said, "You're Toby, right?"

Dumbfounded, Toby nodded.

"You must be Will," he said to Will. He looked at Julian, who gave him a little wave. "And you are?"

"Julian."

I looked from Will to Toby. They both appeared

shocked that this man, who they had never met or even heard of, knew who they were. And to be honest, I was kind of shocked myself. I marveled once again at how much Dad must have talked to J.R. about me. *They'd had an entire life together.* I loved how much Dad had loved me, and I hated J.R. for having had so many conversations with Dad that I wasn't a part of. That I'd never know about. It wasn't fair. Had J.R. known Dad better than I had? Better than Mom had? I wanted to throw something again. I was too warm, and I took off the sweatshirt that I'd been wearing over my Yankees T-shirt for days. How long was I going to feel this way for?

Bob returned to the dining room with a carton of milk and pulled up one of the folding chairs that had appeared in the apartment since Dad had died and we suddenly had all kinds of visitors. "All right, who wants milk?" he asked, unstacking some waxy cups and opening the carton. He looked to J.R. and raised his eyebrows. "You look like you could use something to eat."

"Nah, I'm good. Thanks, though." J.R. sat down between Will and Julian. Will froze.

"So," Bob said, looking around as if evaluating just how difficult it was going to be to get these guys talking. "Who's been following the Yanks?" I couldn't blame him for trying. He didn't know that Will and Toby were just realizing that I'd told them about only a fraction of my life for the past ten months. He didn't know that they were most likely wondering if he and J.R. also had AIDS and that they were probably panicking about catching it by just breathing the air in my apartment.

"I have," Julian said, breaking the awkward silence. "They're really mediocre."

"Yankees fan?" Bob asked.

"No, not yet, anyway. I will be soon, though. I like rooting for the underdogs. Plus my mom and I move around a lot, and I follow all the teams from the cities near where I've lived. So far that's the Tigers, the Mariners, the Phillies...." He looked at the ceiling, trying to remember what team came next on his list, and for half a second, I forgot that Dad was dead and smiled to myself at the fact that, when it came to baseball at least, Julian seemed to have a lot to say. "Oh yeah," he went on. "Then came the Rockies, the Braves, and most recently the Cubs."

"Wow," J.R. said. "You've lived in that many different places?"

"Yup," Julian replied thoughtfully.

"A Cubs man," Bob said. Then he chuckled. "Not sure if we can hang around one another. I went to medical school on the South Side of Chicago, so I'm a White Sox fan. Hey, do you think the Cubs are going to trade Trout for Tewksbury?"

"So are you guys, like, Iris's uncles or something?" Toby asked suddenly, interrupting. J.R. and Bob exchanged a look.

"No, I'm just a friend of the family," Bob said.

"And I'm Iris's dad's ... I *was* Iris's dad's boyfriend." J.R. closed his eyes briefly as if recovering from that sentence. Or possibly to contain the bugs and burning rage associated with Dad being dead.

Will stood up. "Um, so, my parents said that I, like, couldn't stay for too long," he sputtered.

Toby looked relieved that Will had taken the lead. "Yeah," he added. "My mom told me that I should come straight home after giving my condolences. I'm really sorry," he went on. "It's really ... too bad. About Iris's dad."

Julian glanced at me, eyebrows raised as if to ask, *What's up with them?* and the way that he seemed to understand what I was thinking opened a floodgate of anger within me. Will and Toby hadn't even asked me how I was doing. They'd barely even looked at me. *Just shut up*, I thought, envisioning myself standing up, too, and overturning the table.

J.R. caught my eye and smiled just the tiniest bit. A sad, sad smile. The smile said, *Let me help you with that table. It's heavy.* My rage surged into my lungs, daring me to scream. At Will and Toby, who were looking at Julian expectantly, waiting for him to get up. At the doctors and scientists who hadn't found a cure for HIV or AIDS. At everyone in the world who looked down on Dad and J.R. for being sick. And at everyone who looked down on me—who didn't want to be near *me*—because of my connection to Dad. I bit the sides of my cheeks to keep from yelling. J.R. took a deep breath as if to calm himself, too.

"It would be a good decision to make that trade," he said softly to Julian. I understood that he wasn't really talking about baseball but urging Julian not to leave. And I knew J.R. was doing it for me. For my sake. He didn't want me to be totally abandoned. "Bob Tewksbury?" he went on. "He'd be good for the Cubs."

"Yeah," Julian agreed. Then, to Will and Toby, "I'll stay a bit longer. See you at school." And despite the anger in my lungs seeping into my extremities, making them tingle and burn, I smiled at Julian as Will and Toby headed for the front hallway.

"God, I'm tired," J.R. said once the door clicked

shut. He rested his head in his hands, elbows on the table. "I'm just so, so tired." I knew what he really meant was that he was tired because Dad was dead and because so many people didn't have a clue about AIDS. I felt it, too. Everything was too much. There was so much to feel.

"Have you slept?" Bob asked him quietly.

"I can't," J.R. told him. "Is Sarah napping? I have to talk to her. Davis Funeral Home won't even entertain the idea of working with me. We need to find someplace else to have him cremated." Dad had told J.R. that he wanted to be cremated and have at least some of his ashes buried somewhere that would make his parents happy, too—even though Dad wasn't close to them and they would insist that cremation wasn't traditionally allowed for Jews. J.R. shut his eyes and rubbed his hands over his face.

I looked at Julian. He had stayed behind to have a conversation about baseball, but instead, we were discussing Dad's dead body. Strangely, he seemed up for it. He looked from J.R. to Bob to me, concerned. I pictured what he'd say if this wasn't such a terrible thing to talk about. *Won't work with you? Why would a funeral home not work with you?*

"What do you mean *won't work with you?*" I asked.

"Nobody will work with me because we were a gay couple. And besides," J.R. said curtly, "nobody wants him. Nobody wants his body."

I felt like breaking something again. What was wrong with everyone? This was my dad that we were talking about. *My dad!*

Mom walked into the dining room, wiping her eyes. "Sarah," J.R. said. "I've got to talk to you."

"I heard," Mom said as Bob jumped up to get her a box of tissues. "God, I knew this was going to be an issue." Then she looked at Julian. "I'm Sarah," Mom said.

"Julian," he responded.

"Julian just moved from Indiana," I told Mom, as if that were enough to explain his presence at our dining table as we discussed funeral parlors being terrified of handling Dad's dead body.

"I'm so angry," J.R. whispered, looking from me to Bob, to Mom, to Julian. "I'm just so angry that I'm exhausted, but I can't sleep because under the exhaustion is the anger and under that is the fact that he's gone."

I understood exactly what J.R. meant. Julian turned

to me. "It sucks that people can be so judgmental," he said. I got the sense that he wished he could say more. *I'm so sorry, Iris,* I envisioned him continuing. I imagined him reaching for my hand. Smiling at me while taking it in his.

"What are we going to do?" Mom asked.

"Let me make some calls," Bob said. "Neither of you should have to worry about this. Let me take care of it."

"Thanks, Bob," J.R. said as Mom nodded in agreement. J.R. got up from the table. "I'm going to try to get some sleep." Their voices faded into the background as I pictured an endless line of awful men from horrible funeral parlors who didn't want to be near J.R. Who didn't want to be near Dad's body. I wanted to punch them all.

"Everything set for the demo tomorrow?" Bob's voice broke through my swirling, nauseating thoughts.

"All set. Seven a.m., Trinity Church," J.R. answered.

"What are you talking about?" I asked, trying desperately to ground myself.

"It's a demonstration," J.R. said. "On Wall Street. Remember the people who sent the bagels? We organized our first official protest against how the government

92

and pharmaceutical companies are handling HIV and AIDS."

"Is it going to fix anything?" I asked, envisioning a bunch of people just as furious as me marching through the streets, protesting against the unfairness of this all. Against the unfairness of Dad being dead. The image tethered me to my chair. "Will it make a difference?"

"I don't know," J.R. said. "I think so. I hope so. Something has to change. Something has to give. This isn't sustainable."

This *wasn't* sustainable; nothing about how I felt was sustainable. I remembered Dad's thin, dying body in the fetal position in his bed, and then, just as quickly as the image came to me, I shoved it away. I couldn't look at it. It was too terrible. "I want to go to the demonstration. Mom, can I go?"

"Oh, I mean, I don't know, honey. It's not really for kids. I'm not even going." She looked from Bob to J.R. as if to get their input.

J.R. smiled. "It's not *not* for kids," he told Mom. "And remember, Steven had wanted her to learn about the activism. *And* I promise I won't lose her."

Mom smiled a little. She seemed so tired. "Okay," she said, turning to me. "But it's at seven a.m., so you'd better get to bed early." And for the first time since Dad had gotten really sick, I felt the tiniest bit lighter, like maybe there was something, however little, that I could do to make myself feel better.

"Great!" I said. Then I looked over at Julian. I had momentarily forgotten that he was here. Our eyes connected. He looked intrigued. *That demonstration sounds really cool. Can I come?* I imagined him asking.

"Do you want to co—"

"Yeah, sure," he said, smiling, before I could even finish the question.

Chapter Eight

It turns out it's not hard to wake up at five thirty in the morning when you can barely sleep to begin with. By the time the alarm on my clock radio chimed, I was dressed, ready to go, and flipping through Dad's poems. I stopped at one from the beginning of sixth grade that Dad had left under the door not long after he and J.R. had moved in together. Reading the poem made me remember what I'd felt toward J.R. back then: pure hatred. Of course, by writing this poem, Dad had been trying to nudge me away from that feeling; he'd been trying to persuade me to give J.R. a chance.

OPEN *by Steven Cohen*
October 30, 1985

Offer yourself to the maze that enfolds you.
Pardon the mess. Step with curiosity into
Each aperture. Be the eye of the
Needle, the nucleus of the cell.

Now, rereading the poem a year and a half later, I wondered again about Dad and J.R.'s life together. Things had been important to them that I didn't know about, like AIDS activism. They had all these friends who were sending us food and cards, and I'd never heard of any of them. It wasn't fair that J.R. knew things about Dad that I didn't, but at the same time, he felt like a doorway to the parts of Dad I could still get to know. Besides, I was running out of room in my body for feelings, and being mad at J.R. seemed like the easiest one to let go of.

At six fifteen, there was a quiet tap at the door. J.R. let himself in, and I put my empty cereal bowl into the sink. Then we walked out into the dark morning in the direction of Julian's apartment.

It was too early for talking, so we walked along Fifth Avenue mostly in silence. On the corner of Thirteenth

Street, J.R. ruffled my hair. "I'm glad you're coming with me, kid," he said. The cold air smelled like bus fumes, and the awakening city rumbled around us, the sounds of traffic and far-off conversations reaching for us through gray light.

When we arrived at Julian's building near Union Square Park, we found him waiting in his lobby. He waved through the glass of the revolving doors before pushing his way out. "Hi!" he said, way too chipper for early morning. It seemed like he might have been up for ages already, too. His blond curls were damp from the shower, and since he'd be going to school after the protest, he had his leather backpack thrown over one shoulder of his stonewashed jean jacket. Even though it didn't seem right to think about anything aside from Dad dying, I couldn't help noticing the smell of his shampoo.

J.R. led us around the block, and we boarded the subway. By the time we climbed the stairs to street level at Cortlandt, it was almost six forty-five. The twin towers touched the sky behind us, and it felt cold and dark among the narrow streets and tall buildings. As we stepped onto the sidewalk, J.R. put a hand on each of our backs as if to keep us from getting lost. Julian's eyes widened at the chaos and looming old buildings.

"There's Trinity Church," J.R. told us, pointing as we made our way down Broadway toward Wall Street in a sea of people, most of them holding briefcases and wearing business suits.

In front of the church's main doors, a group of protesters with posters and signs was gathered to wait for the demonstration to begin. Most were young men, but there were also women and older people. Unlike at my private school, where there were only a few African American kids, there were many shades of white and brown among the crowd. Did everyone here know someone who was sick? How many of them were HIV positive or had AIDS themselves? Was the anger in my and J.R.'s veins the same as the anger in theirs? Something about them glowed, drawing me closer. Could my feelings be their feelings, too? And what about Julian? I studied his face, noticing the black flecks in his light blue eyes, as he marveled over the church and the crowd. What was he feeling? *Why was he here?*

J.R. wrapped his arm around my shoulder and pulled me tight. His windbreaker smelled like Dad. I closed my eyes. *Hey, Earthworm*, I imagined Dad saying. Then I tilted my head back and looked all the way up to where Julian was looking, past the stained-glass windows of Trinity Church, past the clock with golden hands, past the pointed spire, to the slowly brightening blue-gray sky.

"Hey, kid," J.R. said, his arm still around me, nudging me a little. "Let's go join our people."

As we approached the crowd, a voice called out. "J.R.!" Julian, J.R., and I turned to find two men, about Dad and J.R.'s age, and a young woman, waving. They joined us and handed J.R. a couple of flyers as several police cars pulled up in front of the church, sirens wailing. The loud noise scared me, but J.R. seemed unfazed, as if he had been expecting the police to arrive.

"How are you doing?" one of the men asked J.R. sadly, wrapping him in a hug. He was mostly bald and wore jeans and a black jacket. I noticed some purple spots on his face. Sarcomas. He was sick. He was dying, just like Dad had died. It was so unfair. Anger filled my lungs, making it hard to breathe. As J.R. hugged him back, I read the flyer in his hand.

NO MORE BUSINESS AS USUAL!
COME TO WALL STREET IN FRONT OF TRINITY CHURCH
AT 7 AM TUESDAY MARCH 24 FOR A
MASSIVE AIDS DEMONSTRATION

I scanned through the list of seven demands that followed: the FDA's approval of potentially lifesaving drugs. Something about cruel double-blind studies, whatever that meant. The release of drugs to everyone with AIDS. Affordable drugs. Public education about AIDS. Policy to prohibit discrimination against people with AIDS. A national policy on AIDS.

I didn't understand what most of it meant, but whoever had made these signs was angry, too. That much was clear.

"Oh my goodness," the bald man with the sarcomas said as he stepped back from J.R., his eyes settling on me. "Tell me this is Iris." He smiled an enormous smile that showed a row of perfectly straight teeth. I looked from him to J.R. This guy knew about me?

J.R. nodded. He seemed...proud. "It's Iris, all right," he said.

"You look like your daddy!" the bald man cried out, happy and sad all at once. Then he turned to the other man and the woman beside him. "J.R. brought Iris!" he announced excitedly, as if they hadn't heard the conversation themselves. They laughed, and I couldn't help smiling as the man threw his arms around me. "It's Steven's baby," he said, rocking me back and forth, making me feel like I'd known him forever. Eventually, he dropped his hands to his side and looked at me. "God, I miss your daddy," he said, wiping his eyes on the back of his hand. "I'm Scott, by the way," he told me. "I guess if some weird man on the street is going to run up and hug you, you should at least know his name." I laughed as Scott turned to Julian. "Now, I don't *think* Steven had a son," he joked.

Julian smiled.

"This is Julian, Iris's friend from school," J.R. said as Julian waved.

Then the other man and the woman introduced themselves. Mack was tall with white skin, rosy cheeks, dark hair, and glasses. Under his jean jacket, he wore a blue dress shirt and tie. J.R. explained that, in addition to being a gay man who had lost way too many friends recently to AIDS, he was a lawyer who had offered to answer ACT UP's legal questions.

Carla had smooth brown skin and dark curls to her shoulders. Without saying a word, she beamed and hugged me to her flowered blouse. I breathed in the sweet smell of her perfume. J.R. explained that her sister had recently died of AIDS, and as she squeezed me tight, I envisioned her sitting by her dying sister's bedside just how I'd sat by Dad's. I squeezed her back.

When she finally released me from the hug, she took a step backward and, smiling broadly, looked me over. "My sweet Iris," she said in a heavy Spanish accent, and I didn't mind that she was calling me *hers*. I liked it. It was like we'd known each other forever, too. She tucked my hair behind my ears and wrapped her arm through mine. "You ready to take some action?" she asked.

I nodded. "Yeah," I told her. I was.

"So," Scott said to J.R., putting his arm around my shoulders, "is Iris as brilliant as her dad was?"

"Maybe even more so," J.R. responded. It was weird that Scott knew Dad so well but I'd never even heard of him. He, Carla, and Mack made me feel kind of famous for being Dad's daughter. And I liked them. But at the same time, the familiar feeling resurfaced: Dad had had a whole life that I hadn't known about. Why had these people been allowed to know things about him that I hadn't?

Offer yourself to the maze, Dad's voice whispered in my mind. So I took a deep breath, and I did. "How'd you guys know my dad?" I asked.

"We met him and J.R. a while ago through the gay community in your neighborhood," Scott replied. "A handful of us started meeting a few months back to brainstorm about what we could do to help ourselves, to help others. Your dad was involved in all of that until he got too sick."

"So you guys are part of the activism group?"

"Yup," Scott said as Carla and Mack nodded. "Officially only since about two weeks ago, but unofficially for longer. Small groups like ours have been working together for months. And now we finally have a name: ACT UP."

"Cool," I said, turning to J.R. "So *you're* part of ACT UP?"

"I am," he answered, smiling.

"And my dad was part of ACT UP?"

"He was certainly a part of everything that went into its creation."

I didn't know what to do with that information. What else didn't I know about Dad? That wasn't a question I could ask aloud, so I fumbled for something else to say. "Thanks for sending the bagels" was the best I could come up with. Feeling lighter, I glanced at J.R. He was suppressing a smile, and I knew we were remembering the thud of bread against the dining room wallpaper together.

"Were they good?" Carla asked.

I tried not to laugh.

"They were *great*," J.R. answered for me. "Much needed."

"There is something you are *not* telling us," Mack said, his eyes twinkling.

"So how did you guys come up with the name ACT UP?" Julian asked.

"AIDS Coalition to Unleash Power," J.R. replied. "Do you like it?"

"Yeah, I think it's good," Julian said approvingly. A glittery feeling coursed through my veins, and looking away so he wouldn't see me blush, I smiled to myself at how well Julian fit in and how glad I was that he was with us. When I looked back, I found J.R. studying me, slightly amused. He raised his eyebrows playfully as if to say, *I know what you're thinking about. Or, should I say, I know* who *you're thinking about.*

I stuck out my tongue at him in response as it hit me that, if Dad were the one noticing that I sort of maybe had a little crush on Julian, I would have felt *way* more awkward.

In the time it had taken for me to meet Scott, Mack, and Carla, the gathering outside the church had multiplied and overflowed onto Broadway. Two blue-and-white city buses and a couple of cabs stopped across the street, unable to get through the crowd on Wall Street and Broadway.

I looked around, stunned. There must have been several hundred people now, many holding signs. Some said STOP AIDS. Others had pictures of President Reagan on them along with angry captions. I knew that Mom, Dad, J.R., and Bob complained about the president constantly, but the truth was that—beyond knowing that he didn't care about people with AIDS—I didn't exactly know why.

"Stick together," J.R. instructed, one hand on my back, the other on Julian's, as we stepped into the street. Before we had made it even halfway across Broadway, we were engulfed in the crowd.

"*We are angry! We want action!*" they chanted, their voices pounding in my ears. "*We are angry! We want action! We are angry! We want action!*" Hearing those words and knowing that I wasn't alone in my rage was shocking. In a good way. Surrounded by their shouts, I actually began to feel less anger, not more. All this time since Dad had gotten sick, it had never occurred to me that so many people might feel just like I did. I looked from J.R., Carla, and Mack, who were chanting along with the crowd, to the demonstrators' signs criticizing the government for ignoring AIDS and criticizing the pharmaceutical companies for charging way too much for potentially lifesaving drugs.

I stopped to watch everything that was happening. Julian looked at me in wide-eyed awe while adjusting his backpack. "All these people—this is fantastic!" he said. "It's going to draw lots of attention!" he continued, searching my eyes as if trying to read my emotions, and it dawned on me for the first time that maybe he was here because he wanted me to feel better; maybe he was here because he wanted to *be with me*.

I smiled to myself as three police officers shoved past us. A woman holding a REAGAN GUILTY OF CRIMINAL NEGLIGENCE sign joined the demonstrators, alongside a man holding a YOU SLAY ME, FDA poster. Two more police officers pushed by. Julian and I exchanged a look, noticing how frantic and serious they appeared. We made our way through the crowd toward the action, where several men and women sat on the road holding hands with one another. *"Release those drugs! Release those drugs! Release those drugs! Release those drugs!"* they chanted over and over and over again.

The police approached the protesters, yelling through megaphones and insisting that they stop obstructing traffic and disperse, but nobody got up. The protesters continued their chant: *"Release those drugs! Release those drugs! Release those drugs! Release those drugs!"*

I wanted them to move. The police seemed mad. Really mad. I turned to J.R. to ask him if he thought we should get farther away from the police officers. I didn't think they would arrest kids, but what about him? What about Scott, Mack, and Carla? What would happen if they were sent to jail? But when I looked behind me, J.R. was nowhere to be found. Scott, Mack, and Carla had also disappeared into the crowd. My stomach tightened in panic.

"Where'd they go?" Julian asked, turning in a circle, trying to see over the heads of the adults. Almost everyone was taller than us. A protester yelped, drawing our attention back to the center of the crowd, where two officers had bent over to pick him up, one holding his legs, the other pulling his arms. The protester let out another piercing shriek. Was he screaming in pain? In shock? To draw attention to what was going on? I didn't know. The way he was being picked up looked like it hurt. Was he sick? Should they be more careful with him? I looked around for J.R. again. Where was he?

Several additional police officers stormed the crowd and began lifting demonstrators off the street and shoving them into police trucks. Their yelps pierced my ears. "What should we do?" Julian asked as a couple of women pushed past us, chanting, "*We are angry! We want action!*"

"You don't think they'd arrest *us*, do you?" I asked him over their shouts.

"I don't know," Julian answered. He reached his hand for mine. Someone bumped into me, and I stumbled backward as Julian grabbed onto my jean jacket, my heart racing. I looked around again for J.R., Scott, Mack, and Carla.

"What if J.R. and his friends get arrested?" I asked Julian. "I don't want to get so far away that we can't see what's happening." The image of J.R. being forced roughly into a police truck flooded me with fear. The officers were being too harsh with the protesters. How could they treat people that way? The demonstrators were just trying to have their voices heard, and lots of them probably were sick with AIDS. I thought back to the night before. To Toby and Will and how positive I'd been that, if Dad had died of something else, their response to his death would have been different. If lots of the protesters had cancer or any other sickness, I *knew* that the police would have been way gentler with them.

Julian pointed to some wooden traffic horses that stood in the road where the crowd wasn't as dense. They were within range of the police trucks. "What if we go over there?" he suggested. "We can stand behind those barricades and still see the arrests. That way, we can keep an eye out for J.R. and his friends."

I nodded and grabbed hold of his backpack strap. We rounded the protesters who continued to chant, "*Release those drugs! Release those drugs!*" Frantically, I kept my eyes glued to the police trucks while imagining an officer dumping J.R. inside like a bag of trash. I pictured him knocking his head on the doorframe. Who would help him as he stumbled, dizzy and bleeding?

Who would clean up his blood?

We neared the sidewalk, where a few demonstrators stood holding signs while businessmen and -women rushed by on their way to work. Two men in suits passed, one pointing at the protesters. "Look at those homos," he said, laughing, and for just one second, I squeezed my eyes shut. When I opened them, Julian was watching me, wide-eyed in shock, waiting to see how I'd respond. I tried to clear my head of the word. I'd heard it, and worse, a million times from people at school, especially last year. I'd gotten really good at ignoring it, but now my eyes burned with tears, and I tightened my grip on Julian's backpack.

A man with a sign that read TURN FEAR INTO RAGE passed, and still trying not to cry, I watched him go. Watched *his sign* go. TURN FEAR INTO RAGE. The words struck me like the heart of a poem, and an image of Dad, back before he got sick, landed gently in my hand like a falling leaf. *Hey, Earthworm,* he said, looking around in awe at the demonstration. The sound of his voice was so real, and I wiped my eyes with the back of my free hand. How was I supposed to live without him? The thought was terrifying. The thought of J.R. getting hurt was terrifying.

Turn fear into rage? I already felt rage, and it wasn't helping me.

You'll figure out what to do with the heart of that poem, Dad's voice promised.

Julian pulled me to the sidewalk behind some orange cones that the NYPD had set up. From that vantage point, we could see the huge crowd of protesters as well as the backs of some of the police trucks. We sat down next to a sewer grate, and a dirty paper cup blew against Julian's feet. "Manhattan stinks," he said, never taking his eyes off the police trucks. Despite the waterfall of fear and sadness inside me, I laughed.

"Sewers, garbage, and exhaust," I told him as a police officer pushed another protester into a truck. They must have arrested fifteen or twenty people. "My dad used to say the smell was a malodorous Manhattan melody."

Julian laughed, and for one quick second, I glanced away from the police cars to his face. It was open. Calm. Where do feelings go when your body is so full of them that it's ready to burst?

"Julian?" I asked, looking back to the demo, surprised by my ability to care about so many things at once.

"Yeah?"

"You know how you said that moving around so much had messed with you?"

"Yeah," he answered.

"*How* did it mess with you?" I pressed.

"I don't know." He picked at his fraying shoelace. "You constantly feel like an outsider. And when you finally become friends with people, you have to leave them. I guess it's better just to not get attached."

I nodded, saddened by the thought of him feeling like an outsider. And wondering, despite how different our lives were: Did Julian and I have similar-looking paperweight hearts?

"So why did you want to come to this protest?" I pressed.

"I don't know," he said again, but in a way that suggested that he *did* know but was embarrassed to tell me. I glanced at him, at his suddenly flushed cheeks, and then back to the police officers who were preparing to drive off with some of the protesters. Maybe to jail.

"Sometimes..." His voice trailed off.

"Yeah?" I prodded, looking down at my dirt-smudged shoes and the garbage-littered street—the malodorous Manhattan melody—eager to hear what he was struggling to say.

"I guess the thing is that you can *try* really hard not to get too attached to certain people, but..." He smiled at me. "Sometimes you just can't help it."

When the police cars and trucks had pulled onto Broadway, their sirens wailing, my panic rose. I hadn't seen J.R., Scott, Carla, or Mack shoved into them, but that didn't mean that it hadn't happened before Julian and I got to the sidewalk by the barricades.

Just as I started to feel the fear within me pressing on the backs of my eyes like thickening steam, I heard my name. "Iris!" J.R. yelled from halfway across the street. Carla, Scott, and Mack were with him. "Iris!" he called again, trotting toward us and wrapping me in a hug as Carla threw her arms around Julian.

No longer able to contain hot tears, I managed to say, "I thought you guys got arrested. I thought they threw you into one of those trucks."

"Not this time," Scott reassured me, rubbing my head as J.R. continued hugging me. When he finally let me go, his hazel eyes were damp; he'd been crying, too. In all this time since Dad had died, I'd never seen him cry. Not once. His tears startled me.

I squeezed him again, desperate to make him feel better.

The problem with J.R. was that, in order to hate him, you had to try really, really hard. If you lost your focus for even a minute, you started to love him.

Chapter Nine

CARVING *by Steven Cohen*
November 11, 1985

Craving truth, the core,

A statue to be

Revealed in marble, I pick up my chisel.

> I feel

Vitality in its splintering grip. Relief.

> Join me

In carving? Let's try it. Let's know our

> cores

Need us. Let's find our statues. Let's never

Give up.

I closed the navy binder and placed it on top of the red one. The picture frame that had fallen when I slammed the door was still facedown. The back of the gold frame, its cardboard stand pointing upward, reminded me of the tantrum I'd had right after Dad died, and that reminded me of how much better I'd felt at the protest, surrounded by all those people with the same emotions as me.

I stood in front of my bedroom mirror, brushing my hair and trying to ignore both how tired my eyes looked and the low-grade buzzing of anger in my veins. It was ever present, and I was getting used to it, but that didn't make it easier to deal with. I wished it would leave me alone, just for today. Julian and I had plans.

When I entered the kitchen, partly exhausted, partly furious, and partly excited, I found Mom standing in the middle of the room watching the weather on channel seven. I hoped she wouldn't notice that I'd put on my favorite peach-colored stirrup pants and matching sweatshirt; I didn't want her to know that I couldn't wait to spend my Saturday showing Julian around Central Park. It didn't seem right to be happy about *anything* right now.

But she didn't seem to notice. As usual, she appeared sad, like her whole being was drooping toward the yellow linoleum floor. She was a wilting flower. I wondered if, while I was busy worrying about floating away, Mom was worrying about being dragged by an invisible hand to the center of the earth.

"Hey, baby," she said, smiling a sad little smile. I wished I could fix her; I wished I could make her happy.

"Hi, Mom."

As I'd gotten dressed, I'd read one of the poems I'd written to Dad back in December of sixth grade, over a year ago. I remembered that warm winter day so well. Through gusting wind, Dad and I had walked to our favorite ice cream shop on Broadway. We hadn't even been wearing our winter jackets. Then we'd made our way over to his office so he could pick up some papers. The warm wind had blown my hair into my rainbow sherbet as we'd crossed the street.

TRANSFORMATION *by Iris Cohen*
December 2, 1985

This hasn't been easy.

Right after the divorce, Mom got

Angry. And I'm not talking your normal "I'm

Not happy with this" kind of

Stuff. I'm talking

Fury.

Out-of-control

Rage. Slamming cabinets shut while

Moping (but loudly). Infuriated.

At your office, I picked up

The glass orbs on your desk where

Inside, colorful curves crept.

One day, will Mom's anger calm? What will arise in
its place?

New pinkpurpleperiwinkle curls, coils, arches? Or
something on fire?

He'd responded the next day.

TRANSFORMATION *by Steven Cohen*
December 3, 1985

"Tell me everything," I

Remember urging. Your

Anger inhabited tiny fists, clenched like dark houses.
I tried

Not to laugh (you always

Saw the truth, even then) as you told me,

Fury swelling like a fast-expanding sun,

Of Mrs. Frank, who

Removed you from the art table for spilling yellow
   paint.

Make me the sunshine, Earthworm. Paint me

A lemon boat on an amber sea beneath the autumn
   light.

Take me with you across orange-yellow waves.

Imagine it: fists relaxing,

Opening, palms upward. Sunbeams radiating,
   illuminating the

Night sky. Lighthouses in your hands.

Now Mom snapped off the TV once the weather
report ended and a segment about Ronald Reagan and
Japanese import prices came on. "Do you want some
cereal before you go?" she asked. "Lucky for you, Caroline dropped off groceries, and you know her stance on
sugar cereal." Caroline was a nurse in Mom's practice.
They'd worked together for years. Her kids ate things
like Lucky Charms, and Fluffernutter sandwiches on
Wonder Bread. In other words, foods that Mom would
never buy. I opened the cabinet to find a box of Froot

Loops next to our plain oatmeal and poured a bowl quickly, before Mom could change her mind.

"Tell me about your plan," she said, sitting at the table with me as I stirred the cereal, turning my milk pale blue.

I avoided eye contact with her, feeling awkward for her sake. I didn't want her to think I was going on a date or something. Even though I wondered if maybe I was. "I'm meeting Julian downstairs, and we're going to the park," I told her, which seemed like a simple enough explanation.

She nodded, and I thought that, maybe for a second, I saw a twinkle in her eye. "You have enough money and subway tokens?"

I patted the pocket in my stirrup pants while shoveling a spoonful of Froot Loops into my mouth.

"Be back by dinnertime?" she went on. "Bob is picking up pizza."

"Is J.R. coming over, too?" I asked.

"No, he's having dinner with friends," she said. I wondered, yet again, what purpose Bob served now that Dad was gone.

"What are *you* going to do today?" I asked, slurping the sugary milk. I didn't like the idea of her home alone, moping around the apartment with nobody to keep her company.

But she gestured in the direction of a stack of patient files on the dining table. "I have to catch up," she said. "I'm so behind."

I nodded, preferring the image of her hunched over files to sleeping under the crocheted blanket. "Looks like lots of fun."

She smiled. "Hey," she said, getting up to take my bowl to the sink and tucking a strand of my hair behind my ear, "I'm glad you're getting out."

"Yeah," I agreed, "me too." I avoided eye contact again as a warm feeling flooded me. Then I kissed her goodbye and rode down in the elevator, heart fluttering, to find Julian waiting for me in the lobby.

Chapter Ten

Being in Central Park felt like time travel, and I had to work hard to remember *when* I was. Julian's presence was a string keeping me from floating all the way out to space, but I still felt ungrounded. I had to remind myself that it was Saturday, March 28, 1987. That I was walking down the path near the main entrance to the Central Park Zoo with Julian at my side. That I was pointing to the trees, showing him how the leaves were light green, rust-colored, and pink, saying it didn't make sense that we always thought of springtime leaves as *only* green.

Because while in reality it was almost April, in my

mind it was also winter. January 1986, a few months after Mom and Dad's divorce. I was at the park on a school field trip, and the brown snow was sloshy atop dirty paths and boulders. The primary colors of my classmates' jackets and hats dotted the scene. The sky was gray.

And it was summer. So many summers, folded into a stack of poems, illuminated by a sunbeam. Everywhere I looked, I saw myself and Dad. I was a toddler in his arms, pointing at the bronze statue of the tigress and her cubs, just like in the picture on the wall at home. Then I was a kindergartner climbing a small hill as Dad watched and waved. I was in elementary school, and Dad and I were eating ice-cream cones by the pond, and I was crouching next to a pigeon with him by my side.

I looked at Julian, his blond curls framed by the budding trees behind him. He smiled, his braces reflecting the sunlight, and I wondered if it was ever truly possible to know someone. I mean, to *really* know what was in their head. I tried as hard as I could to will the slushy snow and summer leaves away; I tried to remind myself that it was 1987. Springtime. That it was *now*.

"You better never forget that your first time in

Central Park was with me," I said as the main gates of the zoo came into view, along with the smell of animal poop, trying to bring myself back to reality.

"I'll never forget. I promise," he said, sticking out his pinkie. I wrapped mine around it.

"Does that hilly area over there remind you of Indiana?" I pointed to a knoll that was mostly mud but soon enough would be covered in grass. When I'd finally asked Julian a few days before what Indiana was like, he'd explained that no, he hadn't lived on a farm, but that the town he'd moved from wasn't exactly a suburb either. *It's a small town*, he'd said.

The closest thing to a small town that I knew was Corning, where Dad grew up and where Grandma Bea and Grandpa Fred still lived. We hardly ever talked to them, but I knew that once Bob figured out the funeral stuff I'd have to see them again. I didn't want to. They were cold, stiff, and proper. So different from Dad.

"Well, the hill looks like it's made of mud, and there's some grass on it," Julian said, grinning. "And in Indiana we also have hills made of mud with grass on them, so yes," he teased. "It definitely reminds me of Indiana."

"Smart-ass."

He laughed. "How did you become such a strong person?" he asked, out of nowhere.

"Strong?"

"Yeah, like you're dealing with all these things with your dad and your family, and still, you wanted to go to the ACT UP demo, and you're out and about...." Through the main gates of the zoo, people crowded around the ticket stands in small groups. "Like, you're still going on with your life."

I didn't know how to respond. What did he mean, *going on with my life*? I wasn't going on with my life, and I definitely wasn't *strong*. I looked away, toward the skyline. The thin threads of anger that had woven their way throughout my veins weeks ago were thickening into knotted ropes. I hated Julian's question. He didn't know me at all. I didn't want to go to the zoo anymore.

"Do you want to skip the zoo?" I asked, envisioning a summer breeze blowing to my right, a light snow falling to my left.

"Sure, you're my tour guide," he reminded me, clearly unable to sense my swelling rage.

I turned in a circle, almost expecting to see Mrs. Abbott, my sixth-grade homeroom teacher, and my classmates in their Moon Boots and jackets, mittens and hats. I'd known that it was stupid of me to not just tell the people I'd grown up with that my parents had gotten divorced. That my dad was gay. But I hadn't wanted to, and for five months, I'd gotten away with it. Until, that is, someone had found out and spread the word when we were on our sixth-grade winter field trip to Central Park.

Julian was wrong. I wasn't strong now, and I definitely hadn't been strong back then.

After the field-trip incident, it had taken several days for me to tell Dad that people from school had been making fun of him because they'd found out he was gay. I think that, until then, he and Mom had just assumed that people from school had known everything about their divorce for months.

JERKS *by Iris Cohen*
January 10, 1986

Just as a sea lion was about to
Emerge from the pool,
Randy and Tara were like, "We heard your dad
Kisses MEN! Hahahaha." And I
Stood there, a statue in the snow, watching them laugh.

I wasn't strong. A strong person wouldn't have tried to hide the fact that Dad was gay from anyone in the first place. A strong person wouldn't care what people thought.

———

Just north of the zoo was one of the summerhouses that I loved. It was called Summerhouse at the Dene, and I led Julian to it. "Okay, *this* is something you have to see. For the most part, the only people who like this place are the old ladies and me," I explained.

He laughed. "I wonder what you'll be like when you're an old lady."

"I wonder what you'll be like when you're an old man." I looked down at my shoes as I said it, because an image of the two of us walking side by side in the park, holding hands, had come to mind. But it was stupid. Julian had me all wrong, and you can't marry someone you don't know, because if you do, everything is just a disaster waiting to happen. *That* was something I knew firsthand.

Back when I'd been really little, Mom, Dad, and I would come to the park together as a family. But as time went on, it became more of my and Dad's thing, and I wondered how much of that had to do with Mom and Dad not truly knowing each other.

I led Julian uphill to the summerhouse, which was actually an open structure made of branches and tree trunks with cool wooden benches around the periphery. To the right of the summerhouse were sloped rocks that were fun to climb. I loved how the sun would come through the slats in the roof and stripe the ground with sunlight and shadows.

On the day of the field trip, over a year ago, the benches had been damp. I'd found the driest spot to sit on when I'd finally figured out how to move and left Randy, Tara, and the rest of my classmates at the zoo. Sweaty in my down jacket, I'd been staring out at the buildings on Fifth Avenue, trying to figure out how two stupid sixth-grade girls had so effortlessly concluded that they were better than Dad simply because he was gay and they weren't. That was when Mallory, Will, and Toby had shown up.

"Hey," Mallory had said, because she was always pretty much the leader of the pack. She was tall for a twelve-year-old and wore her brown hair in two tight braids. I'd known her forever, but we'd never been close, because I'd never been part of the "outsiders" group;

I'd never been part of *any* group. I had always just been kind of friendly with everyone.

"Hey," I'd responded, looking back to the skyline.

"We heard what Randy and Tara said," Will had chimed in, and I thought for sure he was going to ask if it was true, but he didn't. He just said, "They're real assholes."

"Yeah, I know," I'd said, smiling a little. I couldn't explain how or why, but Will saying that had toppled the pedestal that I'd put Randy and Tara onto.

"They're total airheads. They cheat on, like, every math test," Toby had added, wiping his dripping nose on the back of his hand. "Even the easy ones," he'd gone on, as if that fact solidified things. "So *definitely* don't listen to them."

I'd looked from Mallory to Will to Toby and felt immediately better. Kind of how I'd felt at the protest—*not alone.*

Julian and I sat on a bench across from where I'd been sitting on that winter day. "This summerhouse thing is awesome," Julian said. "You know, my aunt and uncle have a summerhouse. Like an actual one. It's upstate. My mom and I are living with them now. Did I tell you that?"

I could tell by the way he asked the question that he knew that he hadn't.

"No," I said. "That's cool. Do you like them?"

"Yeah," he said quickly. "Living with them is really good. They're cool and nice, and they're rich compared to us. They're the ones paying for me to go to private school. For years, my aunt tried to convince me and my mom to come live with them, but my mom never wanted to. Until now."

"Oh," I said, suspecting that what Julian was telling me was more important than he was letting on.

He kicked at some pebbles on the ground. "My mom always calls herself a 'free spirit,' unlike her older sister, my aunt Rhonda, who, according to my mom, is a boring lawyer, but I think it's really that my mom feels like Aunt Rhonda is always judging her."

"Oh," I said again, wanting to know more but not sure how to ask without seeming like I was prying.

"I mean, I get that," Julian went on. "It's how I feel when I tell people how much we've moved around. I know people must be wondering what my mom's deal is. It just feels so..." His voice trailed off.

I nodded, ashamed that I'd just wondered that very thing. I understood so well the feeling that he was trying to describe. It was one of the colors in my paperweight heart, and it hurt to look at it. I didn't know what to say. Thankfully, he kept talking.

"Anyway, I don't think Aunt Rhonda is boring. I think my mom just says that because she can't hold down a job for more than, like, six months before getting fired. She's working for my aunt now. As a secretary at her law firm."

"That's cool," I said, wondering if I should ask Julian about his dad or try to find some nonjudgmental way to ask him why his mom kept getting fired from her jobs. Maybe I could tell him that I thought he was brave to move around so much. But then I thought of how wrong he'd been when he'd told me I was strong and how bad that had felt. I didn't want to be wrong about him; maybe he *wasn't* brave. "Well, I'm glad you moved here," I finally said. I didn't mention my worry that he wouldn't stay for long.

"Yeah," he agreed. "I am, too."

"Do you want me to show you something else?" I asked him, sensing that he'd be relieved if I changed the subject. He nodded, and I led him out of the summerhouse. We passed the *Snow Babies* statues, which I used to love. The two stone babies looked so happy sitting on

130

their white chairs, frozen in time. When I was younger, I'd wished that I could shrink them inside a paperweight so I could examine them, solidified in glass forever. Whichever way I'd tip the paperweight in my mind, they'd never move. They'd never stop smiling.

Up ahead was the Waldo Hutchins bench. It was an enormous, curved, white granite bench with Latin words along its back. I used to love running along it. In the fall, leaves would gather on top of the white stone, and I'd crunch through them as Dad would watch, laughing. In third grade, my after-school art class had come to the park with peeled crayons and manila paper to do rubbings. I remembered kneeling on the bench, a leaf stem stabbing me through my red tights, as I'd held my paper over a *V* in *VIVAS* and run my purple crayon sideways over it. I'd shown it to Dad when I'd returned home. "It's from Waldo's bench!" I'd told him proudly.

"You brought home a *V* from *ALTERI VIVAS OPORTET SI VIS TIBI VIVERE*," he'd exclaimed. "Well done, Earthworm." He'd put the paper with the messy purple letter on the fridge with a magnet.

Now there were no dried leaves to run through. I walked along the white bench anyway and thought of

how Dad had responded when I'd told him what happened at the zoo.

ADVOCACY *by Steven Cohen*
January 11, 1986

About Randy and Tara. You shouldn't have to
Deal with them, but you do. Create a
Vision
Of equality, and patiently (these things take longer
    than they should)
Cast it over them like
A net for minnows, or a shadow of hands. You should
    not have to
Carry them forward, but
You have to carry them forward.

After Julian and I ate the lunch he'd brought for us
in his backpack, we walked across the park to the American Museum of Natural History. I was starting to feel
exhausted from existing in so many seasons at once. All
day long, I'd been burning up in the summer sun one
second and freezing in a blizzard the next. Then, in the
blink of an eye, I'd be back in springtime with Julian.

I loved the museum—its huge white stone facade,

the columns, the stairs to the main doorways. I hadn't been in almost a year. When Dad and I had come last June, it had been so hot outside and so cold inside. My favorite exhibit at the museum, even though it was hor-rifying, was the squid and the whale, and I was excited to show it to Julian.

When Dad and I had last been here, just after he'd been diagnosed, we'd stood together for a long time star-ing at the giant, boxy face of the floating sperm whale statue and the massive orange squid that had attached itself to the whale's cheek. The statue didn't make any sense. Whales were supposed to be these enormous, gentle, human-smart mammals, swimming around and enjoying life, but the whale had been attacked by the squid, which was so much smaller than it, and even though the two animals were frozen in time in the museum forever, you still had the sense that this jerk of a squid was going to be able to take the whale down. How was that possible? How could that happen? How could something so small destroy something so powerful?

I thought of all this again while standing on the sec-ond floor alongside Julian, looking down at the squid and the whale. I wondered what Dad had been thinking back when we'd stood here together. Maybe the same thing as me. Maybe something totally different. Now I'd never know.

"Whoa," Julian said, studying the two animals in the diorama. "Who's going to win?"

"The squid," I told him definitively.

"Really? Why?"

I felt angry again. *Why?* Because it was obvious. That was why. How could he not see it?

"I kind of think the whale will win," he went on.

"How's it going to get that squid off its face?" I pressed.

"I don't know," he almost whispered, as if the fight between them were real and, in the end, one of them *was* going to die after all. "I just think the whale will be able to do it."

We exchanged a look, and in that moment, the thick ropes in my bloodstream dissolved, once again, into nearly weightless threads. It was like Julian knew that the battle we were looking at was more significant than two massive fake animals on display in a museum. Maybe he even knew that, in watching the battle between the squid and the whale, I was thinking about Dad.

I wished I could talk to him about it. *This exhibit makes me think of my dad*, I could have said. But he would have asked me for details, and I couldn't get close to the heart of that poem. So instead we were both silent as I wondered about all the things that Julian didn't say in his life and thought about all the things that I didn't say in mine.

Chapter Eleven

RESPITE *by Steven Cohen*
February 20, 1986

Remember at the park last week, how we visited the

Eternally happy *Snow Babies*? You took

Snow, smeared it on your Freezy Freakies, and the

Picture morphed. The smiling penguin appeared.

    Remember? In the

Icy air, I forgot everything.

The sadness I caused vanished and,

Eternally happy for one moment, I *existed*.

Back when Dad first wrote this poem, I got it, but I didn't *get it* get it. Now I understood exactly what he'd meant by a *respite*. From time to time, a few minutes would pass where I'd be distracted from the fact that Dad was dead, and in those moments, life would feel normal again.

It had happened a couple of times at the park with Julian, like when we'd been about to sit down for a picnic lunch and he'd pointed out two scurrying ants on the bench. He'd nudged them onto a napkin to transport them to the grass rather than flicking them away like I would have done, and in that moment of watching the black ants dart across the pink napkin, Dad wasn't dead; I was just existing.

When I'd gotten home, I'd ridden the elevator to the eighth floor and waved to our neighbor, Mo, as he'd come out of his apartment, his tabby cat peeking through the crack in the doorway as he'd closed the door behind him, and it had happened again. I was just alive. Going about my day.

Now, two days later, as Mom and I cleaned up from dinner, I felt desperate for more of it—for more of those moments.

The buzzer rang as Mom handed me a platter to dry. "It's me," J.R. called through the door before letting himself in. "I was on my way to the lobby," he said, hugging Mom and tousling my hair, "but I wanted to drop these off." He put two cards from his and Dad's friends onto the kitchen counter.

"Where are you off to?" I asked, remembering how good the respites felt as I looked around the darkening kitchen, my eyes landing on Mom and her sad, sad eyes.

"The center," he told me. "ACT UP is meeting."

"Cool," I said. "Can I come, too?"

"To an ACT UP meeting?" J.R. asked, sounding surprised.

"I don't know. I'm just so..." I didn't know how to finish. So jittery? So unsettled? So bored? So *mad*?

J.R. looked to Mom.

"Honey, the meetings really aren't for kids," she told me.

"That's what you said about the Wall Street demo," I reminded her. "And that was f—" I cut myself off, because it didn't feel right to say that the demonstration had been *fun*. I mean, people there had been shoved into police trucks. I'd gotten separated from J.R. People there had been sick. Dying. Their friends and family were sick. Dying. Dad had been sick. Dad had *died*. But at the same time, I couldn't help focusing on how much I had liked being there with J.R. and Julian. And how much I had liked Scott, Carla, and Mack. It was weird that something so terrible had also, somehow, felt good. Somehow, parts of it had also felt *fun*. "And that was *fine*," I said.

J.R. smiled at me like he knew what I'd almost said. "Your call, Sarah," he told Mom. "I'm happy to bring her along if you're okay with it."

Mom shrugged. "I mean, I guess it's okay." She looked at me. "There definitely won't be any other kids there," she said.

"I don't care," I replied quickly.

"I promise I won't lose her," J.R. said, just as he'd done before the Wall Street demo, and I avoided eye contact with him because I didn't want Mom to get any hints that J.R. kind of *had* lost me and Julian on Wall Street. We'd decided, while coming home on the subway, *not* to share that information with her.

"All right," Mom said. "I'm okay with it."

"Great," I said, relieved at the thought of getting out of the apartment. I ran to my bedroom for my jacket and shoes.

In the elevator, J.R. gave me a playful nudge. "You're just like your dad," he told me, grinning, and I got the sense that, in that moment, J.R. was experiencing a few seconds of Dad not being dead; he was just *existing*.

"How so?" I asked as the doors opened to the lobby. J.R. and I waved at Mason, the doorman.

"He found peace in being an activist, too," he told me.

I thought about that. Was that what I was doing? Finding peace in becoming an activist?

The air outside was cool, springlike, perfect late-March air. "I didn't know that," I said.

"It was before he got really sick, before ACT UP. A bunch of us would get together, usually at someone's apartment, sometimes at NYU, to talk about what we could do to fight against being actively ignored by the government. Actively taken advantage of by the pharmaceutical companies. He had lots of good ideas for demos, meetings. Grassroots things."

"I didn't know any of that," I told J.R. "Why didn't he tell me?"

"Oh, I don't think he was purposely keeping anything from you," J.R. said as we made our way toward Thirteenth Street. "I think it was just that you seemed younger then, even though it wasn't so long ago. Like, you weren't quite mature enough to fully 'get it' yet."

I nodded, turning that over in my head. We passed storefronts, buildings, and tiny trees growing out of tiny patches of dirt in the sidewalks.

"Having a parent die when you're young forces you to grow up quickly," he went on. "I know that firsthand."

"You do?" I asked, shocked by this thing that we had in common and by how little I knew about J.R.'s family or about his life outside of his relationship with Dad.

"I grew up in New Jersey," he said.

"Oh yeah." I vaguely remembered Dad saying something about that.

"But small-town New Jersey. Kind of farmland, if you can picture that," he said, and my mind flickered to a vision of Indiana. Of Julian. J.R. gently nudged me with his elbow just like he'd done in the elevator. "Yeah," he said, reading my mind *again*. "Probably similar to where Julian used to live."

"Hey!" I joked, nudging him back. "What makes you think I was thinking about Julian?"

"Were you?" His eyes twinkled in the lights of a diner.

"You were saying?" I went on. "About your family's farm?"

He laughed. "When you're born in a tiny, rural town in 1945, and you tell your mom in 1960 that you like boys, usually things don't end well for you. But my mom was extraordinary. She was kind of the opposite of your grandpa Fred and grandma Bea."

"That's so lucky," I told J.R. "How did she get to be so cool? Am I going to get to meet her someday?"

"Unfortunately, no," he said, waving to three men across the street who seemed to be headed in the same direction as us. "She died when I was seventeen."

"Oh, I'm sorry," I said. "For some reason, I assumed you were talking about your dad when you said you'd lost a parent when you were young."

"Nope, it was my mom," he said. "Her death was a loss. A huge loss. After she died, I was completely alone. I felt like I was just bobbing along in a giant, freezing ocean, isolated from everyone and everything. That's when I moved to the city."

"And what about your dad?" I asked.

"Never knew him."

"Siblings?"

"None. It was just me and my mom."

"So you don't have any family?"

"Nobody close," he said. "Your dad was my family."

I wanted to hold his hand, but that would have probably been weird. Instead, I said, "Tell me more about your mom."

"Well, her name was Pearl. She was very independent, very smart. She worked as a secretary at a bank, but everyone knew that she basically ran the place. Of course, despite that, she was still paid a secretary's salary because she was 'just a woman.' She was very open-minded and forward-thinking. I'll never forget the conversation I had with her when I told her I was gay."

"What did she say?" I asked, thinking back to how Grandma Bea and Grandpa Fred had basically stopped talking to Dad when he'd come out and he and Mom had gotten divorced.

"Well, one night after dinner, I just blurted it out. It was eating me up from the inside out, because everything I saw and heard told me that it was a sin. I couldn't keep it in any longer. I said, 'Mom, I'm a homosexual,' and she put down the glass that she was washing and said, 'Jason Randolph Holmes, the world is going to try very hard to convince you that there's something wrong with you, and it's your job to prove *to yourself* that the world is wrong.'"

"So did you?" I asked. "Did you prove that to yourself?"

"I did," he said. "Because of her. And then I gave the same pep talk to your dad. But the older you are when you get that talk, the harder it is for it to sink in."

"Did Dad think he was wrong?" I asked, feeling nauseous at the thought of it. "You know, for being gay?"

"Oh yeah," J.R. said. "It takes a long, long time to rewire what society works so hard to teach you. You need people to help. You can't do it alone."

I stopped walking and looked around. Up ahead, a crowd had formed outside the center. Laughter floated toward us. "Hey, girlfriends!" a man in a white T-shirt called out, running across the street to join the group of men. They embraced him, and another burst of laughter followed.

"I didn't help my dad with that," I told J.R. "I never even thought of it."

"Oh no," he said quickly, hugging me. "That was my job, not yours. He was your daddy. Your job was to feel your own pain. Your family broke."

"You don't think I should have helped rewire society?" I asked, my head buried in the crook of his elbow.

"Nope," he said definitively. "Someday," he added.

"Once you've had enough time to be sad that your daddy died. But not till then."

More laughter burst forth from the group of people that was beginning to file into the center. I wondered what was so funny, and finding out seemed a whole lot better than talking about being sad. "Should we go?" I asked J.R. "It looks like everyone's going inside."

He checked his watch. "Yeah, it's almost time," he confirmed. "Let's do it."

Chapter Twelve

J.R. guided me into a large, open room with scuffed green and black tiles that looked like they'd touched the soles of a million shoes. Mom had been right; I was definitely the only kid there. But like J.R. had said, I felt like a different kind of kid than I'd been when Dad died, just a week and a half before.

The room was crowded, the air thick with the smell of cologne, perfume, and sweat. J.R. led me past a box fan that blew the too-warm air in soft, humid gusts. I took off my jacket and looked around at all the different shades of all the different faces. I listened to voices talking, yelling, laughing. Being there made me feel older, and I liked that. It made me think of one of my favorite poems from Dad.

ANASTASIA *by Steven Cohen*
March 2, 1986

At bedtime, the

Next chapter awaits.

Anastasia, the girl like you,

Suctions poetry from solid surfaces,

Talks to her goldfish through glass. In

An underwater world (ours, but trembling), did a
     duchess

Somehow perforate the glimmering barrier,
     transform into a girl

In conversation with a fish? Did they then (united)
     dive into you?

And what wavering wall will you puncture? Who will
     you become?

I thought about those questions while looking around the bustling room. I thought about glimmering barriers and wavering walls. The exposed pipes in the ceiling, peeling white pillars scattered about, and bulletin-board-studded walls certainly didn't bring to mind anything that glimmered or wavered, but I knew that looks could be deceiving.

At the front of the room was a chalkboard on wheels. On the top, in messy cursive, it said *Monday, March 30, 1987* and listed several people's names. Below them were words and abbreviations that I recognized as possible AIDS drugs: AZT, ribavirin, Ampligen, Glucan, DTC, ddC, AS 101, MTP-PE, and AL 721. Beside the list, someone had written *Over 500,000 dead. Now what?* A group of people who seemed like they might be in charge were gathered together by the chalkboard, talking enthusiastically.

"Jason Randolph," an operatic voice boomed, and J.R. and I turned to find Scott coming our way. His face lit up when he saw me. "And if it isn't Iris Cohen," he added to his melody in a deep baritone.

J.R. clapped as Scott took a bow and kissed him on the cheek before hugging me. "My little Iris Cohen, with a name like an ice-cream cone," he sang as if he were on stage at the Met. I laughed.

Carla came up behind him and whacked him playfully on the head. "You're going to scare her away," she warned. I loved the way her eyes glimmered when she spoke.

"I'm not that easy to scare," I reassured Carla. She threw her head back and laughed like I was a great comedian.

"Good," she said, wrapping her arm around mine. "Because some of the folks here are pretty scary," she joked. "Let me show you around before the meeting starts."

"Wait," J.R. said.

"What's wrong?" I asked.

"Let's make a plan for where to meet. I can't lose you again," he told me. "That would make me the worst..." His voice trailed off, and he laughed a little, but I could tell it was a fake laugh. It was an *I just revealed the heart of my poem* laugh. The worst *what*? Dead-Dad's boyfriend? Leftover father figure? Friend? "That would make me the worst," he repeated, leaving it at that. "Your mom would kill me."

"Sarah couldn't kill a fly," Scott said, swatting J.R. on the arm. "We all know that."

"You know my mom?" I asked Scott.

"I met her once," he told me. "A while back. And your daddy talked about the two of you all the time."

As Carla dragged me away from J.R. and Scott, I thought again about how much I didn't know about

Dad. I hated it but also loved it. It made him feel less gone.

"Okay," Carla said, her arm around my shoulders. "I definitely can't lose you now. Not after *that* from J.R." She winked at me. "You know how loved you are, right?" she asked, squeezing me tighter.

"I guess?" I answered.

"You *guess*?" she said. "Oh, there's Mack." She pointed to the back corner of the room where a bunch of people, mostly men, stood in a circle talking. Some of them wore nice pants and shirts as if they'd come straight from office jobs. The way they spoke to one another made me think of old married couples who argued constantly but also loved each other. They were discussing something about the FDA and Mayor Koch.

"You have to approach it with them as if it's a moral issue," a man in a dress shirt with rolled-up sleeves said emphatically.

"A moral issue?" Mack answered as he spotted us and waved us over. "These people have no morals. They are devoid of morals." A bunch of people around him nodded in agreement, but it was strange: They were talking about the most depressing topic—people who clearly didn't care about AIDS—and at the same time, they didn't seem totally discouraged. They seemed... together. It was just like at the Wall Street demo; maybe the anger had gotten diffused among the crowd again. I mean, I could sense it. It was still anger, but somehow, at least for now, it felt more like *energy*. "More importantly," Mack said, "because really, screw the FDA, this is Iris Cohen, Steve's daughter."

The crowd laughed at his comment about the FDA and turned its attention to me. Several people introduced themselves and shook my hand. Some hugged me. They all told me how sorry they were about Dad dying. One guy congratulated me on becoming ACT UP's youngest activist. I couldn't tell if he was serious or not, but it made me smile.

When they finally went back to their conversation about whose side Dr. Fauci was on anyway, Carla put her arm around me and led me toward the front of the room. "You didn't know this side of your dad, did you?" she asked.

"No," I admitted. "Why does everyone know him?"

"Well, he had brilliant ideas," she said.

That made sense. Dad had been super smart.

"He wasn't the best public speaker," Carla went on. "He was more of a behind-the-scenes kind of guy."

I could see that. Dad was soft-spoken. Kind of quiet.

"He had a way of taking these massive ideas and boiling them down," she continued. "I don't know how to put words to what he would do. He'd take a huge idea and carve away at all the extraneous junk around it and..."

"Identify its heart?" I asked.

She stopped walking and looked at me. Her big brown eyes were teary. "Oh my gosh," she said, smiling and sniffling all at once. "Yes. Just like that. He'd identify the heart."

I wanted to wipe away her tears, but that seemed weird. I didn't like seeing her crying. I preferred the animated energy of the room to her sadness. "It's what poets do," I told her.

"I guess you would know, huh?" she asked, wiping her cheeks with the sleeve of her red sweater.

I shrugged, embarrassed. "I guess so?" I said, smiling, as I tugged her away from where we'd stopped walking, next to a white pillar with a flyer from the Wall Street demo taped to it. "Come on. Introduce me to more people."

"Okay, mini poet," she told me. "I will."

We made our way around the periphery of the

room. Carla pointed out the different groups of ACT UP members, who were informally congregating in various corners. Some were quiet. Others were loud. Some looked serious. Others laughed boisterously as they talked. The faces I saw ranged from white to tan to brown to Black; from female to male; from plain to made-up in gaudy eye shadow and lipstick. There were men in earrings. Men in business suits. Women in dresses. Women in T-shirts. Every kind of person filled the room. Quite a few were engaged in enthusiastic arguments. When we returned to where J.R. and Scott were sitting, I asked them about it.

"Why are so many people in here arguing with one another?"

Carla laughed. "That's how we roll."

"But seriously?" J.R. asked. "It's because everyone in the room has a different passion, and everyone thinks their particular passion and their particular way of being an activist or an ally is the *right way*. Someday they'll learn," he went on.

"Or not," Scott added.

"Or not," J.R. went on, smiling. "Anyway, someday they *should* learn that there are lots of ways to be an activist. There are lots of ways to be an ally. It can be

easy to get self-centered. To forget the overarching purpose. You know, to miss the forest for the trees."

I nodded, thinking about that.

Then Scott turned to Carla. "You ready?" he asked.

"Ready as I'll ever be," she responded.

A man at the front of the room rang a bell and
called the meeting to order. Carla joined him next to the
chalkboard.

"Okay, quiet down!" she boomed. I was impressed
with how her voice carried over all the shuffling as
people took their seats. "We all know the truth: In five
years, at the rate we're going, two-thirds of people with
AIDS will be gone. Dead."

My eyes burned with tears and I looked at J.R. *Was
that accurate?* He looked away.

"So what are we going to do?" she went on. "I want
to talk to you about what I know about peaceful protest
versus taking more combative measures."

For several minutes, Carla went through a list of
things she had learned about peaceful protesting from
her parents' experience in Chile, where she was born.
As she spoke, people yelled out questions. Sometimes
she answered them, sometimes others did, and I loved

everything about what was going on. I loved the way that, just like at the Wall Street demo, my rage monster seemed to calm when I was with ACT UP. I pictured the anger rising out of me and everyone else in the room like fiery, magnetic dust. I could almost see it hovering above us in the air before falling back to Earth, sprinkling all of us equally. The people who had come in with less anger would leave having taken some of mine. The feeling brought me such relief that suddenly, I felt tired. I leaned my head against J.R.'s bony shoulder. He shifted the brown paper bag in his lap and put his arm around me as Carla finished her talk.

When she walked back to her seat in the row ahead of ours to shouts of gratitude and lingering questions, someone else took the floor and began to speak. I couldn't see him with my head resting on J.R.'s shoulder, but his voice sounded familiar. I sat up straighter. There at the front of the room, his NYU Medical Center ID hanging around his neck, was Bob.

Wide-eyed, I looked at J.R. He grinned as Bob continued speaking.

"I've been in touch with my connections in Japan, London, and Mexico City, and I have some new information about a couple of these drugs to share with you.

This information is a starting point only, but some of it will be very useful."

"Bob?" I whispered to J.R., shocked, as Bob went through some hopeful statistics regarding one of the medications that wasn't available in the United States but that could be purchased through the black market.

J.R. winked at me. "Yeah, kid. Bob," he confirmed.

Bob paused at one point, and a woman in the back of the room called out, "Does someone want to start making a list of the possible benefits and side effects of these medications?"

Several voices praised her idea, as did Bob, and then he continued speaking. I watched him. He was short and round, and everything about him, from his appearance to his voice, was curves and soft edges. His personality seemed so different from the loud, visibly angry activists who filled the room. I couldn't figure out what he was doing at an ACT UP meeting.

"Is Bob gay?" I whispered to J.R.

"Bob?" he asked, surprised. Then his face softened. "No, kid. Bob's in love with your mama."

I looked back to the front of the room, where Bob was wiping the sweat from his forehead with a handkerchief. Then he reached into a brown bag, pulled out a vial of medication, and held it up so the audience could see what he was talking about.

Bob's in love with your mama.

As Bob, who some of the ACT UP members referred to as Doc, answered questions from the crowd, I thought back to all the times throughout the past ten months that he'd come over to Dad and J.R.'s. How involved he had been in helping take care of Dad. How much a part of the family he had felt. How had I not seen it? The thought of him and Mom together made me feel weird. But not bad weird.

"Is Mom in love with him?" I asked J.R. quietly.

For a minute, he didn't respond. "That's a tough one," he finally said. "I'm not sure."

When Bob finished his presentation, he joined us in the audience, taking the empty seat next to Carla, right in front of me.

"Thanks, Doc," a couple of people sitting near us whispered.

As someone else got up to speak, he turned around. "I didn't know Toe-ris would be here," he whispered, chuckling at his own joke. An older man in glasses blew him a kiss. Another saluted him, and Bob waved off their thanks.

"How did—" I started to ask J.R., but he cut me off.

"I'll fill you in on the way home," he whispered.

I nodded, then leaned my head back onto J.R.'s shoulder, suddenly overwhelmed by everything in the world that I didn't know.

———————

When J.R. gently shook me awake, the room was cooler and half-empty. Carla, Scott, and Bob were gone. J.R. helped me into my jacket, and we stepped outside into the nighttime air. Half-awake, I stumbled on a crack in the sidewalk. J.R. put his arm around my shoulders. "So?" he asked. "How did it feel to be ACT UP's youngest meeting-goer?"

"It was...interesting," I said. My mind was still stuck on Bob. Because I was so groggy, what J.R. had told me about him being in love with Mom made both more and less sense. On the one hand, it explained why he was always at our apartment. On the other hand, nothing made sense, which reminded me of a game I used to play with Dad when I was little. It was called the *Why are* game. We'd walk down the street and ask each other questions such as, "Why are trees trees?" At first, it seems stupid, but if you think about it, the questions make perfect sense. Why *are* trees trees? Why *are* sidewalks sidewalks? Why *is* Iris Iris? I thought about that as we turned right on Fifth Avenue.

"J.R.?" I asked.

"Hmm?" A crowd of college students passed us on the sidewalk.

"Why is Bob...Bob?"

J.R. laughed. "Because he's a good, good guy," he told me. "Good to the core. Kind of like a superhero."

He didn't look like the superheroes on TV, but I knew what J.R. meant.

"How'd he meet Mom and Dad?" I asked.

"Well, when your dad was first diagnosed, back in June, your mom actually went to Bob," J.R. said.

"She did? Why?"

"She knew of him from work. He had a reputation. He's brilliant. And he's an activist. And an ally. And he knows what it's like to lose someone."

"He does?" I asked.

"A few years ago, his wife died of breast cancer. She got the best care possible, but she still didn't make it. Bob is an empathizer. He'll take your pain and feel it like it's his. *That's* what makes him a superhero."

"Super-Empathizer?" I asked.

"It's a bird! It's a plane! It's..."

"Bob!" I finished for J.R., and we both laughed. I didn't feel half-asleep anymore; in fact, I was pretty wide awake.

Hearing J.R. say all these great things about Bob made me wonder why Mom wasn't in love with him back. "J.R.?" I asked.

"Yeah, kid?"

"It would be good for Mom to be in love with Bob."

"Maybe so, but you can't force these things. Maybe it will happen, maybe it won't. Part of me thinks your mom isn't over the divorce yet."

"Is that why she doesn't come to ACT UP meetings?" I asked.

"She came to an informal gathering a few months ago. It was at Mack's apartment. She's a wealth of medical information, you know."

"Is she?"

"Of course. But I don't know. It's really emotional for her. It's just...overwhelming."

I thought of Mom's sadness and wondered if it could be spread out in the same way that my anger was when I was with ACT UP. I didn't know how it worked with sadness.

At the corner, we stopped under a streetlight. J.R.'s

gray curls formed a silver halo in the glow. "J.R.?" I asked as the light changed and we crossed the street. "What color was your hair? Before..."

"Before I became an old man?" he joked.

"I didn't say it. *You* did," I replied.

"Blond," he said. "Just like your buddy Julian's."

I shot him a look because I could hear the smile in his voice. "My *buddy*?" I repeated.

"Should I call him something else?" he teased.

"I don't know," I said honestly. "It's weird, you know?"

"I sure do."

"Like when we went to Central Park, half of the time I loved him, but not really for any reason. Mostly just because he didn't kill the ants on the picnic bench. Instead he moved them gently to the grass."

"Sounds like a keeper to me," J.R. said seriously.

"Yeah, but then the other half of the time, I felt like he didn't know me. He said this thing about me that was so wrong. He was like, 'Iris, you're so strong.' It was infuriating."

"You're not strong?"

"No!" I said. "Not even close."

"Huh. Well, you had me fooled, too, kid. Can I ask you something?"

161

"'Kay."

"Did you tell him how you felt?"

I scrunched my nose at the idea. I didn't want to have to tell him. I just wanted him to know. "No."

"Don't be too much of a romantic," J.R. told me. "Nobody's a mind reader." I smiled a little, because *he* usually was.

"I guess. But don't you like the idea of someone being able to just know all the important things about you without having to say a word?" I hadn't realized *I'd* liked that idea until it came out of my mouth.

"Of course, but that sounds like a movie or a romance novel. Not like real life. It would let you off the hook too easily if you didn't have to put words to your feelings. But yeah, I remember feeling that way when I was younger. Like with my first boyfriend."

"Oh, tell me about him!" I said, giggling.

"His name was Sam," he said.

"And?"

"We were fifteen."

"And?"

"Gosh, I loved him. It was so different back then. We had to sneak around. If anyone had caught us together, I don't know what would have happened to us. We'd meet in my barn and kiss in the hayloft."

"J.R.!" I said. "That's so cliché!"

"I know," he said, laughing a little. "I loved it."

"Was he..." I didn't know how to ask the question.

"Yeah?" J.R. prodded.

"I don't know how to say it. Was he like you? Like—"

"Proud?"

"Yeah," I said, smiling up at J.R. as we pushed our way through the revolving door of our building. "Proud."

"He was," J.R. told me. We waved at Mason and got into the elevator. "You have to know how lucky I was to have my mom *and* to have Sam," he said, sounding strangely stern. "I was in the top one percent when it came to luck."

"I get that," I said, reminded suddenly of a poem Dad had written called "PRIDE."

J.R. hugged me good night at my door. When I closed it behind me, I heard him wait until the lock clicked before going back to the elevators. Mom was asleep on the couch. I tiptoed to my bedroom and opened the navy binder to the poem that I now knew was about J.R.

PRIDE *by Steven Cohen*
March 29, 1986

Put one foot in front of the other as you

    climb.

Right, then left.

If you're scared, close your eyes. When you get to the

    top

Don't look down.

Everything that matters exists in the

    hayloft.

Thinking back to that old, beat-up room at the center, I wondered if some of the energy that I'd felt there was what J.R. had been referring to and what Dad had been talking about in his poem: pride.

And then I flipped forward in the binder to a poem called "WILLOW." Dad had written it on July 5, 1986, one month after he had gotten sick. I read it again. I thought of J.R. and Sam in a hayloft. I thought of pride. The poem meant something different to me than it had before I'd gotten to know ACT UP. Or maybe it meant what it had always meant, but I was just now realizing how to put words to this particular heart. It made me sad and scared in a way that I wanted to think about more, but that I also didn't want to think about at all. I pulled the page of notebook paper out of the binder, folded it into a small square, and tucked it into my jacket pocket.

Chapter Thirteen

I woke up late on Monday morning, jittery about the fact that, in exactly one week, I'd have to return to school. When I went to the bathroom to brush my teeth and wash my face, an image of Mr. Inglash—his hand on my shoulder, glasses slipping down his nose—barged into my mind. I thought of Toby and Will, frozen at the dining room table, not wanting to breathe my family's breath. Somehow, over the course of the past two weeks, Mr. Inglash, Toby, Will, President Reagan, and the pharmaceutical companies that ACT UP hated had all tied themselves into an angry knot. They were everywhere I looked. I couldn't escape them.

"Mom?" I asked, searching through the cabinets to

see if there was anything sugary left for breakfast. "What do you think about my going back to school in *two* weeks instead of one?"

"Oh, honey," she replied as I finally gave up and put two pieces of wheat bread into the toaster. "We have to try to move forward. Do you think Daddy would have wanted you sitting at home in your room while your friends got to hang out together and learn all kinds of interesting things without you?"

I thought of my classrooms, filled with students. And of all the messages from Mallory on our answering machine that I was ignoring. Mom was right; Dad wouldn't have wanted me holed up in my room.

But that was the thing. I didn't want to stay home and sit in my room either. Not all the time, anyway. I wanted to *do* things. Things that made my fury dissipate. Like go to ACT UP meetings and demos. *That* was what I wanted more than anything else, because it gave me a respite from my rage.

"Fine," I said, "but at the very least, I'm going to the ACT UP meeting tonight with J.R." I put my hot toast onto a plate as Mom poured herself a cup of coffee. While I hadn't told J.R. my plan, I'd been thinking about it since last Monday.

167

"Iris, sweetie, ACT UP isn't for kids," she replied, looking at me sadly.

The pity in her voice made me furious. "Says who?" I asked, the rage monster blinking its eyes open, stretching through my veins.

"It's just...," she went on, and I could tell that she was searching for an explanation. But maybe she couldn't find it because it didn't exist. I knew that she was wrong. *She* was the one who didn't understand; she didn't know how I had felt in that room with other people who were just as angry as I was. So what if they were adults?

I shoved my untouched toast into the garbage and, slamming the apartment door behind me, stomped up four flights of stairs to J.R.'s, where I rang his buzzer. When he finally came to the door, he looked exhausted, and the dark circles under his eyes scared my anger away. "Were you sleeping?" I asked. It was almost eleven thirty.

"Just resting my eyes," he told me, smiling. "Come in."

It felt weird being in his and Dad's place. I'd gotten so used to the hospital bed in the living room. Someone had come to take it away after Dad had died, and seeing the apartment without it was strange. Being there felt kind of like time traveling, like at the park with Julian.

But when J.R. closed the door behind me and I looked closer, I could see evidence of what had happened. Evidence of Dad dying. There were four square indentations in the tan carpet where the wheels of the bed had smashed it down. The IV stand was in the corner, next to a tall plant.

I flopped onto the couch. "Mom doesn't want me to go to the ACT UP meeting tonight," I told him.

He eased himself onto the chair across from me. "She doesn't?" he asked, but not in a *That's terrible!* kind of way. More like in a *Tell me more* kind of way.

"She says it's not for kids."

"Hmm," he said, looking out the window, over the treetops and between the buildings to the river.

"Don't tell me you agree with her," I said. I knew that J.R. understood the anger in a way Mom didn't.

He smiled, his hazel eyes grayish green like his sweatshirt. "Hey, kid," he said. "Your mom's the boss. I'm always happy to bring you along, but I defer to her. Have you eaten?"

"No," I told him, thinking of my untouched toast in the garbage.

"Me neither. Want to walk to Mirza's with me?"

I got the sense that J.R. was trying to distract me

from the ACT UP argument by asking me to step into a memory of Dad at his favorite restaurant, so I nodded. Besides, I was starving.

"Call your mom and ask her what she wants us to bring home for her. I just have to get myself situated," he said, getting a glass of water and disappearing into the bathroom.

"I already know she wants couscous salad, no feta," I called through the closed door.

He laughed. "You're probably right, but you never know. People can change."

I thought about how it used to be so easy to be mad at J.R. Now it was impossible. Then my mind, overflowing with thoughts and feelings, flashed once again to Will, Toby, and Mr. Inglash. "That's true," I said quietly, pretty sure that he couldn't hear. "People can change."

When I returned to school a week later, I tried my hardest to operate like I had in sixth grade. Back then, I'd had no trouble shutting out anyone who had anything negative to say about Dad being gay. But now, everything felt different. Ignoring people was harder. When

Mr. Inglash would look my way, I'd avert my eyes. But then, when he'd return to writing on the chalkboard or shuffling through papers on his desk, I couldn't help studying him through the fog of anger that followed me wherever I went. What was his problem? *What was wrong with him?*

I felt the same fury toward Will and Toby and disappeared quickly into the library at lunchtime so I wouldn't have to listen to their ridiculous, immature conversations. I couldn't even look at them. I couldn't look at anybody. So I didn't.

Except for Julian.

After school on Tuesday, as we walked home together, I kicked an empty soda can on the sidewalk and contemplated, once again, all the things that I'd say aloud if I were truly as strong as Julian thought I was. *I'm so mad all the time,* I'd tell him. *What am I supposed to do with all this anger?*

And I contemplated J.R.'s advice to not expect anyone to be a mind reader, realizing how much easier it would be to have a crush on someone if you knew what was going through their head.

"That science project is going to take forever," Julian finally offered, breaking the awkward silence.

"Yeah," I answered, relieved that he'd at least said something.

"You want to work on it together over the weekend?"

I smiled to myself. "Sure."

He nodded, relaxing a little. "Cool. Are you going to Philanthropy Club tomorrow?"

"Nah." I'd thought about it a lot, daydreaming about the moment when Will, Toby, and Mr. Inglash would walk into the classroom to find me missing and feel terrible about what they'd said and done. And then I'd realized how stupid those fantasies were. Will, Toby, Mr. Inglash—they weren't thinking about me. They were trying to protect themselves from a threat that they didn't understand. Which meant that they were just like the government, just like the pharmaceutical companies. They didn't care about my family. They didn't care about me.

We stopped at the north end of Union Square Park, and a warm, early-spring breeze rustled the leaves on a tree, sending the malodorous Manhattan melody billowing through our windbreakers. "Call me when you finish the math so we can compare answers?" Julian asked.

"Yeah, sure."

He looked at me, then down at his shoes. *I'm sorry everything is so terrible for you*, I wanted him to say.

Help me persuade people to do something. All these people are dying! Maybe it doesn't have to be that way! I'd respond.

"Well, I guess I'll talk to you later?" he finally asked.

"Yeah," I responded. "I'll call you in a bit."

I let myself into the apartment and, out of habit, looked down at the doormat. The absence of a poem made me even angrier than I'd been all day at school. I stomped straight to my room. Dad's binder, open to a poem, sat on my desk. Looking at it made me furious. Everything around me was a reminder of my shattered world, so I crawled under the covers and waited for Mom to come home.

After dinner with Mom, Bob, and J.R., I plopped myself on the living room couch to do homework. My emotions were exhausting, but math was mindless, and I liked that. Plus, once I was done with the odd problems on pages 201 through 203, I'd have an excuse to call Julian. I threw myself into probability as I half listened to snippets of Mom, Bob, and J.R.'s conversation.

"I'll do that for you, Sarah," Bob was saying.

"No, no. I want to. I don't mind," she responded.

"The funeral home is just around the corner from where my appointment is," J.R. added. "We can walk there together."

My eyes burned with tears. No matter where I turned, I couldn't escape my life. I squeezed my eyes shut against Mom, J.R., and Bob's conversation, against my tears, against the pieces of my body that seemed to be floating away again. I tried to focus on the probability that Juan's spinner would land on blue three times in a row. I imagined the whoosh of an imaginary plastic arrow over cardboard as J.R. said, "ACT UP's plan is to meet on the steps of the post office by four thirty."

"What time's your appointment?" Bob asked.

"Four fifteen. It's okay that I'll be missing it. It will probably be a long demo, but I'm tired. I hope there will be a good showing."

I snapped my fingernail against the imaginary spinner in the light-speckled space behind my eyelids, sending the plastic arrow spiraling again.

"How many posters did they manage to put up?" Mom asked.

"Hundreds," J.R. responded.

"I saw a bunch this morning when I went to the Upper West Side to bring the ribavirin to Seth," Bob added. "They look great. The bright pink triangle against the black is perfect. Do they expect the demo to be as big as Wall Street?"

I opened my eyes, the spinner circling through space. What were they talking about, exactly?

"Hard to say. The timing will be great with the mad dash for the post office," J.R. said.

"Thank goodness for everyone who put their taxes off until the last day," Mom added.

I pushed my math book to the side and wandered innocently into the dining room.

"Hey, Eyelash-ris!" Bob said. "Did you finish your homework already?"

"No, just taking a break." I forced a smile in his direction and sat down at the table. "What are you guys talking about?" I asked casually as Mom got up to begin clearing the plates.

"Just ACT UP's next demo," Bob said, stacking the empty glasses together. "They're banking on a crowd outside the big post office in Midtown. It'll likely be mobbed since everyone will be rushing to get their taxes postmarked before it closes."

I nodded, trying my hardest to appear only halfway interested, like I hadn't already heard their conversation. "Are you guys going?" I asked J.R. and Bob.

"No, not this time," J.R. responded. "Bob has a meeting, and I have an appointment."

"Bummer," I replied, itching to get to the phone as my idea came together. "I have to call Julian," I said. "Math homework," I added as an explanation.

J.R. winked at me from across the table, and I couldn't help but think of a hayloft and late-afternoon sun slanting through dust particles. Me and Julian at the top of the ladder. I rolled my eyes at J.R., trying not to smile. I thought of the very last poem that Dad had written for me before his diagnosis on June second, "CONNECTIONS." In my bedroom, before picking up the phone, I turned to it in the navy binder.

CONNECTIONS *by Steven Cohen*
June 1, 1986

Call me, and I'll call you.
Open the door. Come in if you
Need me.
Now, look around. See the lines attaching

Everyone to everyone like green glass energy?

Count your connections. Take comfort in their

Total number, ever-multiplying. They're

Infinite now. A sparkling web of lines over lines,

Over glowing yarn. Electric threads. A cat's cradle,

    then a hammock,

Now a blanket. You can rest in it.

See how it holds you?

Reading the poem loosened the emotions from my body. My anger floated above me. Sunlit dust above hay. I closed the binder and called Julian to tell him the plan: four thirty tomorrow at the post office.

Chapter Fourteen

It was almost four fifteen when Julian and I got off the subway at Penn Station. "This way," I said, pointing down the garbage-strewn street in the direction of the post office. I hadn't been to this neighborhood in ages, and Mom would kill me if she knew I was here without an adult.

Julian kept glancing around, like he was scared one of our parents might pop out from behind a building, but he followed my lead. He'd been quiet at school, and he'd been quiet on the subway. His nervousness was making *me* nervous.

"I still don't get why the protest is at a post office,"

he managed to say, stepping over the crumpled page of a newspaper that had wedged itself into a gaping sidewalk crack. We walked down the smelly street, and the massive building came into view. The post office took up the entire city block. A huge flight of steps spanned its length, and a row of white columns stood like soldiers at the top of the stairs.

I didn't understand what Julian didn't get. "I mean, there will be a crowd there," I said. "You know, people dropping off their tax stuff? And reporters. Because the news always covers dumb stuff like that."

Just like Mom had predicted, the sidewalk and steps to the main doorways were crowded with people rushing to get their envelopes into the mail on time. Reporters with video cameras were conducting interviews with taxpayers. We approached the steps, where a camera operator from channel two filmed a woman in a navy sweater who was droning on and on about how glad she was that she'd gotten her taxes into the mail today. I rolled my eyes. People were dying of AIDS, and channel two thought that *this* was a story?

I turned to Julian to complain just as he turned to me, shocked. "Hang on a minute," he said, his eyes scanning the massive steps. "*This* is the post office?

This *museum* is the post office?" He burst into laughter, and a man overhearing our conversation chuckled as he passed us.

"Don't mind him," I called after the man, relieved to hear Julian laughing and finally understanding what he'd been confused about. "He just moved here from a farm," I added.

"Okay. *This* is the post office?" Julian asked again, trying to make me laugh even more.

Despite my anger at channel-two news and the world in general, I giggled.

"*Now* I get it. Do you have any idea what the post office is like back in Indiana?" he asked, sounding more like himself. His eyes searched the steps.

"Is it a shack in a cornfield?" I asked.

"Close. It's a building on Main Street that's smaller than a classroom at school. For the life of me, I could not figure out why anyone would want to plan an important demo at a place like that. Now I get it," he said again, looking around, wide-eyed. "*Now* I get it."

Down the block, a large crowd was walking in our direction. ACT UP. "Look," I said to Julian, pointing. Dozens of people, many of them holding signs, began chanting. Shouts of "We are angry! We want action!"

and "Act up! Fight back! Fight AIDS!" filled the air. I scanned the signs as the demonstrators got closer. One of them looked like a giant envelope, addressed to President Reagan. Many of the others were black with upward-pointing, bright pink triangles in the center. Beneath the triangles, in white, were the words SILENCE = DEATH.

Silence equals death, I thought. What did that mean? Could it be true that not speaking out about AIDS actually resulted in people *dying*? Maybe if I'd done something sooner—maybe if we'd *all* done something sooner—Dad wouldn't be dead. I couldn't handle the thought of that, of the feeling that maybe Dad didn't have to be gone. But then I thought of everyone with AIDS who wasn't gone yet, and I wanted to join the protesters. I *had* to join them.

"Come on," I said, pulling Julian in the direction of the crowd just as the camera operator turned his lens toward the demo. I smiled, knowing that ACT UP was going to get itself onto the news again; their plan was working.

"Hang on just a minute," Julian said.

"Why?" I asked, turning back to face him as the chants grew louder. *"We are angry, we want action! Silence equals death! Speak up! Speak out!"*

He pointed through the crowd of people making their way to the post office to a woman holding the hands of two crying toddlers. No, he was pointing past her.

There stood Toby and Will. Both were scanning the mob of protesters like they were looking for someone.

Like they were looking for *us*.

Toby turned in a circle, wiping his nose on the back of his hand. Will adjusted his backpack straps and, spotting us, grabbed Toby's arm, pointed, and waved sheepishly. What were they doing here? I was so surprised to see them that, for just a second, I forgot that I was furious at them.

They pushed their way past the lady and her crying kids. "Hey," Toby said once they reached us. "This place is packed. That's good, right? Julian told us that would be good."

"Yeah, the more the merrier, right?" Will added, looking at his feet and then, finally, at me. "That's what Julian told us, anyway."

I didn't know what to say. I looked at Julian. He smiled and shrugged.

"So," Toby said, taking a deep breath and exchanging a look with Will, "we're sorry."

Will nodded in agreement. "We're going to make it up to you," he said. "Are you still really mad? It's okay if you are. We'd understand."

My mouth didn't work. I looked from him to Toby to Julian, trying to put together everything that must have happened to lead to this moment.

"Oh," Will went on, unzipping his backpack. "I made something for you. For all of us, actually." He pulled out five slingshots made of tree branches and thick pink rubber bands. "Here." He held one of them in my direction. "Your very own catapult." It was the strangest and best gift I'd ever received. I took it.

"The thing is, we were, like, really shocked to learn about your dad," Toby told me nervously.

"We didn't know anything about AIDS," Will added as the chants behind us grew louder.

"So I just taught them some stuff that I'd learned from Ryan White's story," Julian chimed in. "How you can't catch it through casual contact. That kind of thing."

"And we're sorry," Will said.

"Very sorry," Toby added.

"We didn't know," Will went on. "About anything."

"And we're going to make it up to you," Toby

183

continued. "We want to help you. With the protesting and stuff. It sounds cool."

"Say something!" Julian finally yelled at me, smiling. I hadn't realized that I'd been standing there frozen.

I laughed in relief. "Okay!" I said. "It's okay. Thank you." I was so flooded with feelings that I had to study my slingshot for a while because I was scared that I was going to cry.

Toby looked at his watch, and Will stood on his tiptoes, peering out over the crowd, still clutching the remaining four slingshots. "Yes!" he exclaimed suddenly, tugging on Toby's arm. "Look!"

Toby jumped up and down in an attempt to see over the heads of the expanding crowd of protesters. I looked from him to Will to Julian, who had a giant grin plastered on his face as all at once Will and Toby beamed and began waving excitedly to someone. Confused, I followed their gaze.

Mallory was pushing her way through the swarm of people toward us.

Warmth rushed through my body. I watched her toss her long braids over her shoulders, smile, and wave. For the briefest second, I felt like she had never moved. Then it was like I was seeing her for the first time in centuries. Will and Toby seemed extremely proud of themselves, and Julian watched me in anticipation. I couldn't help thinking of everything he'd had to do to arrange for this moment. And then I thought back to his original plan to not get attached to anyone in New York. He was failing spectacularly. The thought made me want to hug him.

Mallory's voice reached us through the mob. "Excuse me! Pardon me! Coming through!" she repeated to the demonstrators standing in her way as she approached. Finally, after what felt like forever, she stopped in front of me. "Your mouth is hanging open," she said, smiling.

I closed it, feeling again like I might cry.

Then she hugged me. "You could have told me," she whispered.

I nodded.

She squeezed me tighter. "I wouldn't have judged you," she added.

"I know." I did know, but I also knew that somehow, for reasons I couldn't explain, telling her would have been impossible.

I wiped my eyes and took a step back to look at her. She was the same Mallory she'd always been, freckles across her nose, wisps of brown hair escaping her braids, yellow backpack over her shoulder. But our friendship felt different, like she was *really* seeing me. I liked it, and I realized how tiring it had been to hide this part of my life from my friends for so long. I'd missed being together with *all* my fellow outsiders. And having Julian with us now? That made everything one hundred times better.

"So?" I asked, suddenly laughing. "How did you...? I mean, *what are you doing here?*"

"A few Sundays ago, when you hadn't called me back for *three weeks in a row*, I called these losers to find out what was going on," she said, grinning and raising her chin in the direction of Will and Toby, who were still smiling proudly. "They told me about your dad. I've been so sad for you, but I didn't want to bother you. I figured you'd tell me when you were ready. But then, they called again last night and told me about this demo."

"We told her everything so you wouldn't have to," Toby chimed in.

I nodded, relieved, wiping my eyes again.

"So," Mallory continued matter-of-factly, "I told my mom that I was taking the train to Penn Station, with or without her. But it turns out that she thought it was a good idea, so I left school early, and we took the train in. I told her no way was she coming with me to the demonstration because I'm *thirteen*, so she warned me like one hundred times that this isn't a very safe neighborhood and to be careful, and then she went to Macy's to kill time. I have strict instructions to meet her outside the main doors of Penn Station at exactly five forty-five or I'm grounded for life."

I looked at my watch. It was already four forty-five. The crowd had multiplied since the five of us had started talking, spreading itself out on the steps. Several newscasters pointed their cameras at the protesters. Police officers, billy clubs in hand, stood in a row, looking on sternly. The chants were growing louder. "Act up! Fight back! Fight AIDS! Act up! Fight back! Fight AIDS!"

"So," Will said to us, "are we protesting or what?"

"Yeah," I told my friends. "We're protesting. But we have to stay in the back. I can't be on the news. My mom would kill me. I'm not supposed to be here."

"Yeah, we know," Toby said nonchalantly. "Julian told us." Then he, Mallory, and Will made their way toward the crowd, and I turned to Julian.

"You did all of this?" I asked him.

"Yeah," he said, smiling at his feet.

I nodded, trying to get my voice to work.

"I did it for you," he went on. "And for your dad. And as a way to try to make it up to you for not saying anything to those guys at the Wall Street demo. So often, I wish I could speak up about things. You know, when you know what you *should* say, but you can't say it?"

I studied his blue, blue eyes, knowing exactly what he meant about speaking up, but confused about one thing. "The guys at the Wall Street demo?" I asked. "Which ones?"

"You know, they were walking by as we were waiting for J.R. to find us?"

I tried to remember.

"The *h* word?" Julian prodded.

"Oh!" I said. I'd forgotten about that; I was so used to hearing that word—and worse—that it hadn't stood out when I'd heard it on Wall Street.

"I wanted to say something to them," Julian went on, clearly distraught. "But I couldn't. I mean, I didn't know what to say, and they were, like, adults, you know?"

"Yeah," I told him, too shocked by what he was

telling me and by everything he had done for me to say more. "I know."

"I just wanted to make it up to you. To let you know I'm with you."

"I know." I did. I knew.

"You guys coming or what?" Mallory yelled excitedly from several steps above us. She, Toby, and Will were already holding black SILENCE = DEATH posters that someone must have given to them.

"Let's go," Julian said, and together we made our way up the stairs through the crowd.

As the five of us neared the back of the swarm of protesters, I felt my shoulders relaxing. It was happening again. The anger was lifting. Leaving me. I knew it was only temporary, but I reveled in how free I felt when it was gone.

An African American man holding a stack of SILENCE = DEATH signs made space for us on the step. "Welcome!" He handed me and Julian posters, and as we took them, I noticed the man and Will exchanging a nod. As the man returned to chanting "Silence equals death!" I thought once again about how Will might feel at school, surrounded by so many people who were white. And I wondered if it was something he'd ever want to talk about.

Mallory put her arm around me. Even though we were standing behind a bunch of much taller people, we held our signs high. I waved mine in the air, picturing the currents it created as it fanned the collective anger. Julian stood to my right, and Mallory, Will, and Toby to my left. I listened to my friends chant, "*We are angry! We want action! Act up! Act out! Fight AIDS!*" Having them there with me made something about Dad's death feel different. The feeling reminded me of when Mallory, Will, and Toby had approached me in the Summerhouse at the Dene in Central Park over a year before. Feeling terrible while surrounded by friends was way less awful than feeling terrible alone.

A lady with rosy cheeks and red hair and SILENCE = DEATH written on her T-shirt in black marker pushed through the crowd. She was handing out baggies filled with . . . something. I didn't know what. "Baby protesters!" she exclaimed when she reached us. "Welcome!" She handed us each a baggie and moved on, continuing to distribute whatever it was that she was distributing. Mom's voice wove its way into my mind. *Oh, honey, ACT UP isn't for kids.*

"What *is* this?" I asked Julian, Mallory, Will, and

Toby, who looked equally confused. I examined the handful of square packets in the baggie.

"Oh," Will said as he took one out of the bag, his lips pursed long after he finished speaking. I didn't know what was going on, but he looked hilarious as he stood, frozen, holding the white square packet between his thumb and forefinger as if it were poison.

Toby took a closer look in his baggie and dropped it on the steps. "Ew," he said quickly.

Next to us, the man Will had exchanged a nod with laughed. "Throw them into the crowd with us. It's a way to protest the lack of accurate information being disseminated about HIV and AIDS. There are ways to prevent HIV, but the government won't openly share that information. It's a travesty."

I took out one of the square packets with *condom* written on the wrapper and almost dropped it, too, but instead I laughed.

"So you want us to just throw these?" Julian confirmed quietly, his face bright red.

"Just throw them," the man replied. "They won't hurt anyone," he added, sensing our reluctance. "They might even save a life."

Toby squatted down to where his baggie sat on the step. "You can do this, Toby," he said to himself as we all cracked up. "You've got this." Then he pinched the bag delicately between his thumb and forefinger as if trying not to touch too much of it, stood up, and wiped his nose on the back of his hand.

"Hey!" Will said suddenly, removing the four remaining slingshots from his backpack. "I almost forgot!"

"Oh yeah!" Toby shouted, no longer scared of his baggie. He grabbed one of the slingshots and enthusiastically loaded a condom into the rubber band. Will handed a slingshot to Julian and one to Mallory.

Julian, Mallory, and I exchanged a look, shrugged, and placed condoms into our slingshots as well, pulling back the pink rubber bands as far as they'd go.

"On the count of three!" Mallory yelled as the adults nearby chuckled. We pointed the condoms toward the people climbing the steps to the post office. "One, two, three!"

We sent the white square packets sailing through the air, laughing hysterically. The rage left my body like air escaping a balloon. The condoms didn't make it very far—not even halfway to where the people were—but it caught their attention. One man even came over to investigate. He picked up one of the white packets from the step, chuckled, and gave us a thumbs-up. In that moment, I felt only happiness.

Hiding behind the crowd from the cameras, the five of us took out another condom each from our baggies and, in unison, shot them in the direction of the people approaching the post office. Watching the little white squares sail through the air, framed by the General Post Office in the background, was fun. *Really* fun. It had been so long since I'd laughed this hard. *Dad would love seeing me like this*, I thought as Will propelled a condom all the way to two women who were walking up the steps.

"David and Goliath," he mumbled to himself proudly, pulling another packet out of his baggie.

I high-fived him just as Julian tugged on my T-shirt anxiously. "Iris!" he said sharply, pointing into the crowd of protesters. "Isn't that Carla? And there's Scott! You're going to get busted!"

My heart jumped, and I looked where he was pointing. Sure enough, through the crowd of ACT UP protesters, I spotted the two of them, both holding signs and chanting enthusiastically.

"Guys!" Julian yelled to Mallory, Toby, and Will,

who were about to release their condoms. "We have to move, or Iris is going to be in *big* trouble!"

"Crap!" Toby yelled in response. "Wait a second. Why?"

"Those people over there know us! They'll tell her mom that she was here," Julian said.

Will looked around, planning our route. "Follow me!" he said, taking the giant steps two at a time, slingshot in hand. I remembered his unenthusiastic instruction to "climb the mountain" in Dungeons & Dragons. The game was coming to life, and it was much more fun this way.

At the top of the staircase, the five of us sat, panting and laughing, our backs against one of the white columns. "Flinging condoms is extremely important, but not as important as Iris not getting grounded," Will announced, and we cracked up again. My side hurt from laughing.

"Thanks, Will," I told him. I wondered if you were exempt from groundings for a while when your dad dies.

"But you know what they say," Mallory added mischievously.

"What *who* says?" Toby asked.

"You know, *them*," Mallory went on. "*They* say . . . it's important to have the high ground."

The five of us exchanged looks and then, simultaneously, loaded our remaining condoms into our slingshots. "On three!" I yelled as we pointed them toward the crowd. "One, two, *three!*"

The little white packets sailed through the early-evening air, through the mist of happiness that had swirled in. I knew the anger awaited me at the bottom of the steps, but the only thing surrounding me now was joy. It was all the colors of the most luminous glass paperweight. Swirls of deep ruby and speckles of hot pink. Yellow firecrackers and a spray of lime green. All those colors and all that happiness reminded me of ACT UP and the people who were *living* despite all the dying. Through the swirls of color and the sound of Mallory's, Will's, Toby's, and Julian's laughter as they watched an old woman pick up—and then immediately drop—a condom, floated Dad's poem from June 2, 1986. It was the poem that he had written for me once he'd gotten the cold that hadn't gone away, and he'd gone to the doctor with J.R., where he had gotten the diagnosis. He had AIDS, and he was dying.

DIAGNOSIS *by Steven Cohen*

June 2, 1986

Deep down

In the deep downs of

Any type of ocean where nothing

Grows where

Nobody goes

(**O**ther than those who have to)

Small creatures still glow

Iridescent. I'm

Sorry. Iris. I'm so sorry.

Chapter Fifteen

Mallory looked at her watch. It was five forty. "I've gotta go," she said. "Talk on Sunday?"

I nodded, smiling.

"And come out for a sleepover soon?"

"Definitely," I told her. "And Mallory?" I paused. "Thank you."

"Iris." She squeezed my arm. "I wouldn't have missed this for the world."

And then, as quickly as she'd appeared, she was off, waving ferociously and pushing her way through the crowd. When her yellow backpack disappeared fully from sight, I thanked Julian, Will, and Toby a hundred more times and said goodbye to them, too. I knew I might get in trouble, and I knew I should leave with them, but I couldn't, so I fished a quarter out of my pocket, walked to the pay phone on the corner, and called J.R.

Now I sat on the post office steps a little ways down from the demo so Scott and Carla wouldn't see me. ACT UP continued to chant, candles in hand, as dusk fell. With my slingshot in my lap, I folded and unfolded the poem "WILLOW" until I spotted J.R. coming my way. Maybe I looked like that rare iridescent fish in the deep downs of Midtown, sitting there all alone. Slowly, J.R. climbed the steps and sat beside me, panting. I tucked the poem back into my pocket, and for a while, neither of us spoke. Part of me wondered if I was going to be in trouble, and part of me didn't care. I was filled with so much happiness and so much sadness.

"J.R.?" I asked. "Remember back when Dad first got sick?" Of course he did. I knew that. I just wanted us to remember it together.

"Yeah," he said, knowing that was all I needed to hear. "I remember."

I put a tiny pebble that was next to my shoe into the

slingshot and shot it down the empty steps. It bounced on the sidewalk before disappearing from sight.

"Cool slingshot," J.R. said, smiling at me.

"Yeah, thanks," I told him. I knew that he'd appreciate the condom story and that he wouldn't share it with Mom if I asked him not to, so I told him everything, starting with how Julian had organized it all. He laughed in all the right places.

"You're lucky to have good friends," he told me when I finished.

"Yeah."

"Did you know that we're not too far from where your dad and I had our first official date?" J.R. asked.

"Really?" I thought back to the time when I was filled with so much hatred for J.R.

"Yeah, we went out for dinner and to Baskin-Robbins for ice cream in Hell's Kitchen."

I nodded, trying to imagine it. I wondered if Mom and Dad were separated at that point, or if Dad and J.R. had gone on a date while they were still married. I wasn't sure if I actually wanted the answer to that question.

"What do you think, kid? Ice cream for dinner?" J.R. asked.

My heart leaped at the thought of going somewhere that had been important to Dad that I'd never been. "Definitely," I said.

———————

At the bottom of the steps, we turned left and walked past Penn Station.

"So, how much trouble do you think I'm going to be in?" I asked J.R., imagining Mom's expression once she found out where I'd been. I reminded myself that it had been worth it to fling condoms from slingshots on the steps of the post office with my friends.

"Oh, your mom doesn't know anything," J.R. said, leading me left on Thirty-Fourth. "I just told her that you and Julian called from a pay phone at the zoo and that I was going to meet you to grab some dinner."

I studied the side of his face, noticing the dark circles beneath his eyes again. "Really?" I asked.

"Really, kid. So tell me," he continued, changing the subject. "How are things with Julian?"

I couldn't stop the grin from spreading across my face.

"That good, huh?" he asked playfully.

"I don't know," I said. I told him the story about the man saying the *h* word at the Wall Street demo and how it hadn't fazed me but had such an impact on Julian. "It seems important that he wanted to make up for not defending Dad. And you."

J.R. nodded, opening the door to Baskin-Robbins. Inside, the light was dim, the air thick and sweet. "You know what you and Julian have in common?" he asked as I peered into the glass case filled with brown cardboard canisters of ice cream.

"What?" I asked.

"Neither of you is willing to be a bystander."

I'd never thought of that before. I liked the idea of it. "I guess that's true. I mean, how can you be, if staying silent results in people dying?" I asked, thinking of the SILENCE = DEATH signs.

I had to look away once I said that. If I'd known about this sooner, if I'd spoken up sooner, would the government have listened? Would the pharmaceutical companies have listened? Would Dad still be alive? Or was AIDS bigger than any of that? I studied the light green of the mint chocolate chip, J.R. by my side.

"It's something that your dad believed in, too," he went on. "Especially once he was sick and he fully realized the gravity of this...thing. He was adamant that he couldn't be a bystander."

"You too," I said. "You're like that."

"I guess you're right," he told me. "I guess it's a thread that unites us all."

The thought of that—of being part of the green glass web that included Dad and J.R., Julian, Mallory, Will, and Toby—made my heart calmer. I put my arm around J.R. while looking over the ice cream flavors, suddenly starving.

"So, what's it going to be, kid?" he asked.

"Butter pecan in a cone."

"Just like your daddy."

"Yup," I said, smiling. "How about you?"

He rested his head on mine for a second before squeezing my shoulder. "Nothing for me," he said, and my mind flashed to the Mediterranean restaurant and how he hadn't eaten there either. And then I pictured the paperweights on Dad's office desk.

When Dad had been sick, his condition had been up and down. For months he'd be exhausted, thin, lying in bed, coughing, and then he'd get better. Maybe not all the way better, but better enough to seem like himself again. It was during one of those stretches that I'd written the poem about the paperweights.

PAPERWEIGHT *by Iris Cohen*
December 20, 1986

Please don't forget

About the

Paperweight museum. Remember how we thought

Every paperweight was

Really someone's heart?

We wandered around,

Examining the poem

Inside each orb of

Glass. Remember

How we wondered which of

The hearts were ours?

After J.R. paid for my cone and we left the ice cream shop, we walked around the block to a tiny park under a streetlight with benches and a couple of sad, weed-filled flower beds. J.R. was quiet, and I was getting a weird feeling. Part of it was his silence, and part of it was frustration that, now that the demo was over, my anger was returning. I touched Dad's poem in my pocket. I didn't really want my ice cream anymore, but I licked it anyway as it melted down the side of the soggy cone, sensing that, as soon as I finished, the glass dome surrounding me would shatter.

"So," J.R. said, once I finally finished and threw the sticky napkin into an overflowing garbage can, "earlier today your mom went to pick up your daddy's ashes."

I nodded, but my brain pushed against the very idea of it. Of Dad as tiny particles. I knew he was dead and gone, but thinking of him as dust made me dizzy. "Okay," I said, lying down on the bench, watching the shadows on the concrete sideways. J.R. took off his sweatshirt and made it into a pillow for me. He rested his hand on my back.

"We'll drive up to Corning tomorrow to bury some of them in the cemetery by Bea and Fred's house," he went on. "There will be a little ceremony."

"Okay," I said again, trying to focus on the dirty grains of wood of the park bench to keep myself from dividing into ash like what remained of Dad's body. It was hard to stay together in one solid piece. My body wanted to separate. It wanted to float away.

Often, when I selected a really good word as the heart of a poem for Dad, he'd respond with that same heart, but when it came to "PAPERWEIGHT," he wrote three months' worth of poems for me before reusing it. He finally wrote his version almost exactly a month ago, on March 18. His handwriting was weak. Barely legible. It had been the day before AZT was approved, and two days before he'd died.

PAPERWEIGHT *by Steven Cohen*
March 18, 1987

Pieces of my heart

Are

Peeling away. Iris. They're

Evaporating, purple ivy to purple dust

Red water to air. I try to scribble them onto paper. The

Weight of everything. Wait.

Eventually, everything

Is pulled back to earth by

Gravity. Look for my glass

Heart. When you find it, put it in your pocket.

Take it with you.

Chapter Sixteen

The drive to Grandma Bea and Grandpa Fred's took forever. When I was younger, we used to go up to see them a lot. We hadn't visited since before Dad had told us he was gay and he and Mom had gotten divorced. Now that seemed like a lifetime ago.

It was a cloudy morning, and sitting in Bob's car, looking out at the gray sky, made me sleepy. J.R., who was beside me in the back seat, looked tired, too. As soon as we got out of the city, he leaned his head back and closed his eyes, his right hand atop the wooden box on the seat between us that contained a portion of Dad's ashes, his left hand loosely grasping a paper bag in his lap.

Mom looked back at the two of us every now and then from where she sat in the passenger seat. The radio was off, and nobody was talking. The only sounds were the hum of the engine or one of us shifting in our seat. I leaned my forehead against the window in the closed-in quiet and felt the rise and fall of the car over gentle hills. I watched the light green of spring-time farmland emerge and disappear behind bends in the road. The scenery passed by through the fog of my breath on the glass. Even though it had been almost two years since I'd been on this road, I recognized the landmarks as we passed them: the crumbling barn just before the exit advertising tractors for sale, the McDonald's next to the abandoned tomato stand.

About three hours into the drive, Mom switched places with Bob so he could rest. By the time we exited the highway and drove down the little country streets into Corning two hours later, I was so exhausted from sitting and doing nothing all day that I didn't even feel like getting out of the car. Or maybe I didn't want to get out of the car because I didn't want to see my grandparents.

At the stop sign just before their condo, Mom paused for a longer-than-necessary amount of time.

Bob and J.R. both started to wake up. She turned to look at me, and I knew with certainty when our eyes met that we were thinking the same things: *Do we have to do this? Do we have to be nice to them? How could Dad have been so different from his parents?* Then we both laughed a little because each of us knew what the other was thinking.

Bob stretched when he heard our laughter. "Did I miss a good joke?" he asked groggily.

"Fred and Bea don't approve of laughter. Or happiness. Get it all out of your system before we see them," J.R. said, his eyes still closed.

Mom and I laughed harder, and J.R. smiled before opening his eyes and stretching. I felt slightly less exhausted knowing that when I saw my grandparents, at least I'd have Mom, J.R., and Bob with me. It would be four to two. Four people with love in their hearts versus two people made of ice.

I'd never been able to understand how Dad had been created from a mixture of Grandma Bea and Grandpa Fred. I mean, he'd resembled them physically, but the other parts of him—the parts that mattered—seemed like they must have come from some other family entirely.

Mom finally took a deep breath, turned right, and pulled up in front of the condo that my grandparents had moved into once Dad had left home to go to college. The house that they used to live in, where Dad grew up, was only two blocks away. Before the divorce, back when we'd visited them a lot, Dad and I would always walk together to his old house. It was light blue with a wraparound porch. There was a willow tree in the huge backyard, hidden from the house by a little hill. We would sneak over to the willow from the side yard. The space next to the trunk, hidden by the dangling branches, had been his hiding place when he was little. I'd always understood why he'd wanted to hide from his parents. Even before he and Mom had gotten divorced.

Mom parked the car in front of the condo, and I got out, jittery despite my leaden legs. All that sitting partly made me want to run around, while the other part of me just wanted to sleep. The sun poked out from behind the clouds, and I squinted, my eyes not used to the light. Bob got out of the car next. He scrunched his nose as he studied the outside of Grandma Bea and Grandpa Fred's building. Then he rolled his eyes. Despite everything terrible going on, I giggled.

J.R. must have still been half-asleep, because Mom

opened the car door for him and helped him out. Then he and Mom and I joined Bob on the sidewalk. None of us wanted to be there, and with that thought, the lead in my legs loosened. It was just like at the ACT UP meeting—feeling terrible with other people who felt terrible about the same thing dispelled the bad thoughts, at least for a while.

"Well," Mom finally said, "no time like the present."

Bob put his arm around her shoulder. She leaned into him, and J.R. nodded in agreement. I pushed my bangs out of my eyes and rang the doorbell.

It seemed to take a long time for someone to buzz us in. When we finally entered the tiny lobby, the smell of the building overwhelmed me. Dad once told me that the sense of smell evokes the strongest memories, and as the elevator door closed behind us, I almost expected to see a younger version of myself in its mirrored walls, rather than the current me in a crumpled jacket with circles beneath my eyes and messy hair. I remembered being little and leaping over the narrow gap between the tiled floor of the lobby and the dirty carpeting of the elevator because I was scared that I was going to fall through the crack. I remembered feeling giddy about the bowl of licorice that Grandma Bea and Grandpa Fred always used to keep on their coffee table.

But of course, I didn't care about any of that stuff anymore, and I grew madder and madder as the elevator rose. Despite having had two years to get over the fact that Dad was gay, according to Mom, Grandma Bea and Grandpa Fred had barely made any progress.

When the elevator doors opened on the fourth floor, J.R. seemed kind of weak with sadness, and Mom steadied him with the arm that wasn't around Bob. I walked ahead of them to the last doorway on the left. Before knocking with the brass knocker, I looked back at them to gauge whether or not they were actually ready for this. Mom smiled at me, and I looked from her to Bob to J.R., taking them in.

Bob's jeans were frumpy, his sneakers old and worn. His soft belly pushed his green sweater into a gentle hill. Somehow, despite the fact that we'd just been sitting in the car all day, his hair where he wasn't bald was disheveled, and I felt a sudden warmth toward him. Toward the way that his arm was around Mom's shoulders so tenderly.

J.R., who was kind of leaning into Mom, was a mess. For a second, I had to look away from him. His tan pants hung loosely on his narrow frame, and he seemed to shuffle a bit as he walked, as if picking up his feet properly took too much energy or required some level of happiness that he just couldn't muster with Dad's ashes awaiting their burial in the back seat of the car. He clearly still wasn't eating; his eyes looked kind of sunken in his face. When we'd stopped for lunch on the road, he hadn't ordered a thing. Not even a glass of water.

And between him and Bob was Mom. Her unbrushed hair fell in soft curls. I liked it that way. When she and Dad used to get dressed up to go out on some Saturday nights, it made me uncomfortable seeing her with makeup on and her hair done up. She didn't look like herself then, but now, strangely, she looked just like she was supposed to. Our eyes connected, and I wondered if she knew everything I was thinking. Not just now, but always.

She gave me a little nod as if to say, *Go ahead and knock*. So I did.

My heart thumped nervously in my chest as I waited for someone to open the door. J.R. put a hand on my shoulder as if to steady me. Footsteps approached, and the door swung open.

"Iris," Grandma Bea said, trying to smile. She and

Grandpa Fred stood side by side, dressed in black for the funeral. What did they think of the four of us, in our frumpy, wrinkled clothes? This was the kind of thing that being around Grandma Bea and Grandpa Fred brought up; they made you question things that in any other situation you'd never worry about. Sitting on the couch behind them was a man with a dark beard wearing a navy yarmulke, a suit, and sneakers. Mom had told me that his name was Aaron and that he was in rabbinical school. Grandma Bea and Grandpa Fred hadn't been able to find an actual rabbi to officiate a ceremony for someone who had been cremated *and* had died of AIDS.

Grandma Bea wiped her eyes with a piece of tissue from her blouse pocket. Then she said my name again. "Iris." Tears trickled down Grandpa Fred's wrinkled face, and they shocked me. Was he crying about Dad? Because he missed him? Because he was disgusted by him? Because he was, by association, disgusted with me?

"Look how grown-up she got," he told Grandma Bea.

I felt stunned by his words, and then, watching the

tears continue to drip down his face, I felt sad for him. I remembered how he'd taught me to play Go Fish when I was little, the card deck on the coffee table between us. Being with Grandma Bea and Grandpa Fred in their open doorway made them seem like real people again.

Real people who were embarrassed by their son because he had been gay. Real people who had told their son not to visit them anymore, hoping that their disapproval would persuade him to change his mind about who he was attracted to. How could they have done that? Didn't they know it didn't work that way? I didn't care about Grandma Bea's red-rimmed eyes or Grandpa Fred's tear-streaked face. Fury torched the inside of my body, and the sudden pain of the flames made me mean.

"Are you happy now?" I asked them. "You don't have a gay son anymore."

Grandma Bea gasped.

"Iris!" Mom cried. My eyes burned, and I felt J.R.'s hand tighten on my shoulder. I stepped back toward him as Aaron appeared next to Grandpa Fred.

I don't care what they think, I told myself. *They started it. They rejected Dad, and now I'm supposed to be nice to them?* But I was shaking. I hadn't realized that I was going to say that aloud. That the rage was going to roar out of me like a beast.

"Funerals," Aaron said. "Emotional times. You've had a long drive. Come in." Grandma Bea and Grandpa Fred exchanged a look, maybe about me, and then moved all the way into the living room as we entered. I noticed that their eyes locked on J.R. as he walked in, and despite the fact that they'd never met him, I was sure that they knew who he was. I wiped my eyes, furious at myself for crying in front of everyone. Furious, in general.

It seemed like Grandma Bea and Grandpa Fred knew that they should give us hugs but didn't want to. Awkwardly, they came a bit closer to us, and finally Grandma Bea embraced Mom stiffly. "Sarah," she said, wiping her eyes, "I'm so sad that it came to this."

Mom didn't know what to say. "It's—" she started, and then stopped, and then started again, as if recognizing that she'd never be able to say anything that Grandma Bea would be able to understand. "It's fine, Bea."

Bob cleared his throat. "I'm Bob," he said, waving to Grandma and Grandpa. "Nice to finally meet you. My condolences."

"Sorry, Bob," Mom said. "I'm distracted. Fred, Bea, meet Bob."

They exchanged another look as if to ask one another, *Is this a boyfriend?* Not long ago, I might have reacted the same way, but now I felt protective of Bob. I hoped he *was* Mom's boyfriend. I wiped my eyes on my sleeve over and over, trying to stop the tears that continued to spill onto my face.

"And you know about J.R.," Mom said, her hand on his back. Simultaneously, Grandma Bea and Grandpa Fred stepped backward onto the rug, and my anger flared again because of how sad I felt for J.R. and how much I loved him.

"Don't you know that you can't get it through cas—" I started, but J.R. squeezed my shoulder again and scrunched his nose as if to say, *Nah, not worth it*. I leaned my head on his bony arm.

"Well," Aaron chimed in awkwardly, "you made good time. It's about four o'clock now. Can I suggest that we head to the graveyard? It's just about ten minutes away."

Mom cleared her throat. "Maybe we'll just use the bathroom quickly?" she asked. "Fred? Bea? It's been a long drive."

"Oh, of course," Grandma Bea said awkwardly. She looked from Mom to J.R. again. "Soap and towels are in the...Actually, I bought some new paper towels." She disappeared down the hallway and came back with the roll, which she took into the bathroom. When she came out, she had the hand towels with her. "I'll just—" she began, fumbling.

"You can't g—" I began. This time Mom gave my arm a squeeze to shut me up.

"I'm going to go to the bathroom and wash up," she said, shooting me a look as if warning me to keep my mouth shut.

Grandma Bea and Grandpa Fred sat down on the couch with Aaron, and I turned my attention to J.R. and Bob. They were talking quietly as J.R. rustled through the brown paper bag that he'd pulled out of his jacket pocket. He took out a baggie filled with orange pills.

"I think try taking four and a half of them this time," Bob said quietly. Mom came out of the bathroom, the hair around her face damp as if she'd splashed herself with water. J.R. turned to go in. And as he walked away from us and from Grandma Bea and Grandpa Fred, I could see it—how, for just one fraction of one millisecond, something in him shifted, causing him to become an almost imperceptible shade less vibrant. Less *him*.

But then, he snapped to his senses and lifted his chin. And that was J.R. J.R., who was proud and had been loved for who he was.

I wondered, again, how Dad had survived his childhood.

In the bathroom, water ran and the toilet flushed. When J.R. was done, Bob and I took our turns freshening up before heading out the door and down the hallway. As we waited for the elevator, Aaron suggested that we take two shifts so everyone would fit. I rested my head gently against J.R. because of how tired he seemed, and because I wanted to protect him from the meaning behind Aaron's words.

When we got outside, Grandma Bea and Grandpa Fred got into Aaron's car, and we got into Bob's. I pulled Dad's ashes onto my lap as Bob backed out of the parking spot. I knew these weren't all of Dad's ashes, but I couldn't stand the thought of *any* of him being left behind here in Corning, in this terrible place where he'd grown up.

In the reflection in the car window, I could see my eyes, puffy and red, and the box on my lap. Behind me, intermingled with the trees lining the road, was J.R.'s reflection. Together, we traveled along like that. The breeze through the windows, the trees, my angry, puffy eyes, J.R., and Dad's ashes.

"Why—" I began.

"Dad wanted this," Mom reminded me gently from the front seat. " 'They're terrible people, *and* they're my parents.' That's what he'd say. He told us to do this."

"I know, but it doesn't make sense. Why should they get any part of him? It's not right." I took a deep breath, trying to steady my voice. "It's not fair."

"It can be tricky with parents," J.R. said, eyes closed again, head resting against the window. He sucked in a deep breath as if even talking about it was hard.

"If they'd been different, if they'd been like your mom, imagine how Dad's life could have been," I told him. Then I looked down at my dirty pink shoes and fingered the folded poem in my jacket pocket. My mind flashed to Central Park. To the *Snow Babies*. To the smell of Dad's jean jacket. To the messy stack of papers waiting to be graded on his desk in his office at NYU.

To his acrostic poems, each one constructed around a beating heart.

Earthworm.

If Grandma and Grandpa had been different, which parts of his life as I knew it would have existed?

Bob drove us past Corning's little downtown area and onto the hilly road that led to the cemetery just out of town. When we arrived, Aaron, Grandma, and Grandpa were waiting for us near the columbarium. We walked slowly so J.R. could keep up.

The grass beneath my feet was squishy and damp, and around us, it stretched out until it touched the surrounding trees. The gravestones were placed in haphazard rows. Some were made of pinkish stone, others gray, others black or white. Some were huge; others were small slabs on the earth like stepping-stones, half-covered in grass. To my right was an arch with a Star of David on it, indicating the Jewish side of the cemetery, while to my left, at the entrance to the Christian side, there was a house-like structure with a cross on top. If you thought about it, it was too much—all the anger that must have hovered over the cemetery throughout the years.

The columbarium was a circular structure surrounded by two steps. Inside were shiny black bricks engraved with names. I knew that Dad's ashes would somehow end up behind one of those bricks. None of this seemed like him. The cemetery, the columbarium, everything felt so...sad.

Right there, next to the steps, with no preamble, Aaron pulled out a small black prayer book. Grandpa Fred was already wearing a yarmulke, and Aaron reached into his jacket pocket, producing one for Bob and one for J.R. "You can keep them," he said quickly, holding them out. My face flushed as my fury swelled; it was hot enough to blow up the graveyard. I wiped my eyes again and again with my sleeves.

And then, Aaron started in with the prayers. I'd been to my great-aunt Hannah's funeral a few years before, and it had seemed a whole lot different than Dad's. For one thing, there were people there. Friends and family. Where were Grandma Bea and Grandpa Fred's friends? Where were my aunts, uncles, cousins, and grandparents from Mom's side of the family?

At Aunt Hannah's funeral, there had been prayers, followed by stories about what she had been like when she was younger. It had been sad, but it had also been happy. Her kids and grandkids had spoken, and once the coffin had been lowered into the ground, we'd taken turns shoveling dirt onto it as if to help bury her.

Almost as soon as Dad's funeral started, it seemed that it was over. Aaron tucked the prayer book into his coat pocket. "My condolences," he said. Then he removed a pair of yellow rubber dish-washing gloves from his briefcase. "I'll take the ashes now."

Shocked, Mom, Bob, and J.R. exchanged looks.

"You can't get it fr—" I began, but this time I shut myself up, and instead of talking, I watched J.R. hold out the wooden box. His pale, shaky fingers touched the dark wood that touched what used to be Dad, and Aaron took the box with his bright yellow rubber gloves. Gloves that should have been alongside a kitchen sink, not carrying the box filled with Dad's remains. What I was feeling—it was too much and everywhere, and nothing was real. I sat down on the grass, the ground cold and damp through my blue jeans, and Mom sat next to me as Aaron thanked us and walked off to a small office, holding Dad's ashes as far from his body as possible. I tried to take a breath, but I couldn't. So much anger was rushing out of me so quickly, like that time at the school playground when I'd fallen onto my back from the swing and gotten the wind knocked out of me. There was no anger to feel and no air to breathe.

"Mom," I whispered.

"Iris."

"It's hard to breathe."

"I know," she told me, crying.

Grandma Bea and Grandpa Fred watched us, arms around each other, but they were like the blurry people in the background of a photograph. Unrecognizable. I thought of Aaron. How he didn't even know Dad. He had no idea that, before Dad had gotten sick, each night before bed, he'd peel an orange over the sink and eat it with juice running down his wrists. He didn't know how the next morning, the orange peels would be there, making the kitchen smell like an orchard. He didn't know how Dad would grade papers only with a green pen because he was worried that red pens seemed mean. How he always brushed his teeth with hot water even though I told him over and over that that was weird. How he always wanted to have a pet parrot that could talk. *Those* were the important things. *Those* were the things that someone conducting your funeral should know.

I started to cry again, but the tears felt different.

"Oh, Iris," Mom said, wiping my cheeks with her sleeves. "It's overwhelming, isn't it?"

"What is?" I asked.

"The sadness."

Chapter Seventeen

For a while, we sat there together by the columbarium. Me, Mom, J.R., and Bob. We watched Aaron emerge from the office, carefully peel off the rubber gloves, and toss them into the trash can by the parking lot. Once he, Grandma Bea, and Grandpa Fred drove away, finally, Mom spoke up. Her tone said, *We're not dwelling on this.* "So, what's the plan?" she asked.

"The plan," J.R. responded from where he had lain down on one of the steps to the columbarium, "is that we're going to drive back to town. We're going to check into the hotel. Then, assuming that Iris is okay with it, she and I are going to take a little walk." I nodded as he went on. "Then we're going to eat dinner, get a good night's sleep, wake up in the morning, and we're going to go home."

"Perfect," Mom said, sounding relieved that by this time tomorrow we'd be back in the city.

We got into the car. At Bob's direction, J.R. swallowed one more pill from his bag. Then we drove to the little hotel about a block from Grandma Bea and Grandpa Fred's that we always used to stay at. While J.R. and I waited on a bench, Mom and Bob brought our bags up to the two rooms we'd reserved—one for Bob and J.R. and one for me and Mom. Then, after Mom double- and then triple-checked that I was okay with her and Bob going off on their own, the two of them walked into town to, as Bob put it, *wander around a bit*.

J.R. turned to me. "So, kid," he said, grinning weakly. "You up for a little breaking and entering?" I smiled back. Whenever we'd go visit the willow in his old backyard, Dad would refer to it as "breaking and entering." It seemed that he'd told J.R. about it. I didn't mind that. In fact, I kind of liked it.

Even though we were only a block and a half from

Dad's old house, it took us a while to get there because of how exhausted J.R. was. Thankfully, there were no lights on in the house; it didn't look like anybody was home. Dad always used to joke that when you were breaking and entering, it was important to walk with purpose, like you belonged. *Remember this in case you want to pursue a life of crime when you grow up*, he'd tell me, and I'd laugh.

"Walk with purpose," I reminded J.R., figuring that Dad had probably taught him the same lesson.

"Always," he responded as we slowly climbed the gentle hill and approached the willow tree behind it.

I loved the willow for the same reason that Dad always had. It was like a little house. A hideout. The branches dangled so low that many of them brushed the ground. When you parted them and walked inside, you were concealed from the world. I understood now, in a deeper way than before, why Dad had needed a hiding place when he was growing up.

J.R. must have been thinking the same thing, because as he eased himself onto the ground, breathless from the walk, he said, "Your dad brought me here shortly after we met. He wanted me to see where he'd grown up, but we didn't visit your grandparents. He said it wasn't worth it and that he didn't want to see them, anyway. We walked around. We came here. He took me to your favorite place, the Museum of Glass, to see the paperweights. Even though I understood it, I still couldn't wrap my brain around his relationship with his parents. I think of my mom so much. I miss her every day. Now that I've met your grandparents, I get it. Now I can see why he didn't want to visit them."

"I wonder if they'll change. I don't know if I'll ever see them again," I said, running a thin willow branch through my fingers. "I don't think I want to," I admitted.

"You don't have to decide right now."

I nodded and put my hands in my pockets, feeling the folded poem, noticing that J.R.'s hands were in his pockets, too. He pulled out a tiny gray sealed bag.

"What's that?" I asked, even though I already knew.

"I felt like part of him should be buried here," he said, tears welling in his eyes.

I nodded.

He found a sturdy stick and handed it to me. I took it and started to dig a hole in the dirt. I didn't feel the same kind of sadness as I'd felt at the cemetery. I was sad, but I was also okay, because I knew that Dad would have wanted to be underground with his willow roots surrounding him. The wind blew, sending the branches swaying and the sunlight flickering like warm raindrops. I liked being enclosed in a dome of green under the willow with J.R. The bad and the good existed together. It reminded me of all the things that I still didn't know about Dad.

When the hole seemed deep enough, J.R. handed me the gray bag and I tucked it into the dirt. What would happen to it? Would earthworms burrow into the plastic, coating themselves in Dad's ashes, spreading them in their paths as they slid through dirt underground? Would the grass and weeds and flowers that emerged be coated in a dusting of him?

"J.R.?" I asked, tears forming rivers on my cheeks.

"Yeah, kid?"

"Can I show you something?"

"Anything."

I pulled Dad's poem out of my pocket, where it had been collecting wrinkles for days, and handed the square of paper to him. He unfolded it and gently smoothed it out.

WILLOW *by Steven Cohen*
July 5, 1986

Windblown willow branches filtered
Icicles then light, icicles then light. I
Lived beneath a dangling dome
Longed for a childhood do-
Over,
Wondering, always, what could have been *if…*

"It's a nice one," J.R. said when he finished reading it.

He didn't get it, and part of me was disappointed.
But I thought again about how he'd taught me that you
can't expect people to be mind readers. That you have
to say aloud what you need. "If he got a do-over…If
Grandma Bea and Grandpa Fred were like your mom,
everything would have been different," I explained.

"I know," he agreed.

"He wouldn't have had to hide."

"Nobody should have to hide."

He was so right that I started crying again. "J.R.,"
I said. "His life would have been happier, and I—" I
knew I had to put words to this heart, but it was so hard

to say it aloud. I steadied myself. Forced myself to say it. "I wouldn't exist."

"Oh, Iris," he said, scooting next to me and pulling me close. "I don't know what to say," he finally admitted. "I never thought of it that way."

How could he have never thought about it that way? Even though I hadn't found the words to put to that beating heart until very recently, the thought, I realized, had been buzzing in my veins alongside the wavering anger and growing sadness ever since the divorce.

"I guess I wouldn't be here with you, in that case," J.R. said quietly.

"But you'd still *exist*. Which would he have chosen?" I asked, not bothering to wipe my eyes anymore. "A lifetime of being himself? Or me? Because for him it *had* to be one or the other." I knew it was an impossible question, but I needed the answer. I needed to hear J.R. say it, even if what he told me wasn't true.

"He would have chosen you," he said quickly, because he understood everything, the heart of every poem, and he knew it was what I needed to hear. He was a poet, like Dad had been.

I nodded, even though the question still existed in

my heart with as much force as it always had. Carefully, J.R. refolded the poem, and I put it back into my pocket. "He would have chosen you," he told me again, this time with such conviction that I wondered if maybe he did believe it to be true.

I forced myself to take deep breaths and wiped away my tears. Then we gently filled the hole with dirt.

For a little while, we sat there together with Dad's buried ashes. "I think he'd like it down there," J.R. finally said. "He always liked bugs and stuff. And earthworms." He smiled, nudging me.

"Yeah," I agreed, remembering the time I'd found a spider in my bedroom and Dad had scooped it into a cup so we could bring it outside and release it on the sidewalk.

"You know," J.R. went on, "there was something that your dad and I disagreed about once he started writing those acrostics for you."

"There was?" I asked.

"Yeah. Your dad told me how the two of you used to joke about acrostics being the most ridiculous kind of poetry."

"In their modern fo—" I began. J.R. cut me off, smiling.

"Yeah, yeah, 'in their modern form, they *are* the most ridiculous kind of poetry.' That's just what your dad used to say."

"Well," I said, giggling, sensing that J.R. was about to challenge me and Dad, "they are."

He shook his head. "They're not," he countered.

"Are too."

"Nope."

"Fine," I said, sifting bits of dirt between my fingers, giving in. "What kind of poetry do *you* think is more ridiculous?"

"Limerick," he said quickly, grinning.

I thought for a moment, scrunching my nose. I didn't like to be wrong, but J.R. might have been onto something. "Limerick, huh?" I asked, continuing to mull it over.

He laughed. "I swear, I had this exact conversation with your dad. I think he even scrunched his nose and said, 'Limerick, huh?' just like that when I challenged him."

"He did?" It made me feel warm inside to know how similar I was to Dad.

"Yes, and then I recited the most famous limerick for him in order to convince him: *There was an Old Man with a beard, Who said, 'It is just as I feared!—Two Owls and a Hen, four Larks and a Wren, Have all built their nests in my beard'!*"

I laughed. "It's really terrible," I admitted. "You might be right."

This was how Dad's funeral was supposed to feel: happy and sad all at once. The two of us talked and laughed until eventually, J.R. began to cough. And then he coughed and coughed and coughed.

Chapter Eighteen

The next morning after breakfast, we decided to extend our stay by a couple of hours. J.R. and I had said that we couldn't leave Corning without going to the Museum of Glass. Mom told us that it made her too sad to think about how much Dad and I used to love it there, so she and Bob dropped us off at the front doorway and then went for a walk along the river.

"When your dad brought me here, he led me straight to your favorite gallery," J.R. said as he bought our tickets.

"Really?" I asked. J.R. was walking pretty slowly,

and he didn't look so great. I wondered if he'd taken his medicine yet that morning.

"Yup. He told me about the heart game."

I felt kind of embarrassed, but also happy, that J.R. knew the game. Dad and I would pretend the paperweights were people's hearts and then make up stories about what each person's life would have been like based on the shapes, colors, and swirls within them.

In the gallery, soft morning sun shone through big windows, illuminating the cases of paperweights. The entire room was sunlight and glass and brightly colored orbs. J.R. and I looked down into the first display case. I remembered these paperweights, especially the largest one with the fiery red-orange explosion in the center surrounded by tentacles that faded from dark, pine-needle green into the color of leaves on willow branches. Around the tentacles, purple droplets hung, transfixed in the orb forever. It reminded me of everything beautiful and everything terrifying existing in the world, all at once.

"J.R.?" I asked, my eyes glued to the paperweight. "How'd you get HIV?"

For a while, he didn't respond. But finally, he did. "I had a boyfriend a couple of years before your dad," he said. "Alex. He didn't know he was sick. Nobody knew anything back then. I mean, we barely know anything now, so how could we have? Iris, you know that I didn't know I had it when I passed it on to your dad, right? You have to know that."

I nodded. I knew J.R. would never have done it on purpose. For the first time, I wondered if Dad had been mad at J.R. for accidentally infecting him. "Are you mad at Alex?" I asked.

"No," he said quickly. "He didn't know. And besides," he continued quietly, "it's hard to be mad at a dead person."

I looked around at all the cases of paperweights. At all the multicolored hearts. "J.R.?" I asked again. "How many people do you know who have AIDS? Who have died from it?"

He looked around, too, as if taking in a gigantic number of dead, beautiful souls. "So many, Iris. Too many to count."

I couldn't understand it. I couldn't comprehend how all these people had been dying all around me for years and I hadn't even known about it. How was it still happening? I was so mad, but my anger felt different now. Less frantic. I was a more thoughtful kind of furious. I wanted to do something, but I wanted to do it the right way.

I led J.R. to the next display case. The paperweights inside were my favorites. Each was filled with flowers. One contained hundreds of tiny white lilies rimmed in blue and dotted with yellow specks. In another, deep purple petals appeared to be frozen in time in an underwater current. "Look," J.R. said, pointing to the garden of purple petals. "Irises."

He looked so thin. His eyes were too big in his head, and his cheekbones protruded. His face worried me and, without thinking, questions tumbled nervously from my mouth. "Why do you think some people get sick so quickly but other people don't? I mean, you're doing pretty okay," I went on. "Right?" All the sunlight burning through the windows was making me too warm. I looked down at the lilies. The irises. And next to them, an explosion of pink peony.

J.R. took a deep breath, and then another. I didn't want to look at him. At his face that so closely resembled Dad's face near the end. I blinked, and tears fell onto the glass. "Iris," he said gently, his voice pleading with me to open my eyes. To look. To see everything that was beautiful *and* horrifying. To see that he was dying.

Even the day before, my instinct would have been to smash everything, but I didn't want to do that anymore. I wanted to open the display cases one by one and gather the hearts. I wanted to collect them all. But they were so delicate, and there were so many. There were too many to hold.

J.R. must have known what I was feeling because he walked slowly around the display case and put his arms around me. I listened to his real heart beating through his shirt as he hugged me. "All these hearts," he said. "They're so breakable. This whole world—"

I nodded.

"I'm sorry," he whispered. "I'm sorry that everything is so fragile."

Chapter Nineteen

The whole way home, J.R. slept, curled on his side in the back seat, his gray halo of hair next to my leg. I thought in paperweights. In glass orbs. I wanted to capture every tree, every valley of flowers, every crumbling barn. I wanted to lower a sphere of heavy, spotless glass over the four of us in the car, preserving us like this forever.

I thought of the feeling I'd had in the museum. The calm rage. And I wondered what to do with it. As we neared the city, beneath a darkening sky, an idea came to mind, and for the first time in a long time, I didn't dread the thought of returning to school after the weekend.

On Monday afternoon, when the three o'clock bell rang, Julian, Will, Toby, and I pushed through the double doorway and onto the playground. "Yes!" Julian said, pumping his fist in the air. "I love our plan!"

"Dude, calm down," Toby responded, sneezing in the sunlight. "Everyone's going to think you're a total dork. We have reputations to preserve!" He sneezed again. "Is it cottonwood season?" he asked, looking around at the tufts of white fluff wafting through the air. "I'm so allergic."

Julian, Will, and I exchanged a look, trying not to laugh.

"Anyway," Toby went on, "we have a *lot* of planning to do."

"Relax," I told him, unzipping my jacket and tying it around my waist. "It'll be great."

"What I don't understand," Julian said to Toby and Will as I opened the playground gate, "is how you guys knew that we should go to Stiffio with our proposal. I mean *Stiffio*? I never would have imagined that *she'd* be with us on this."

"Dude," Will said, pulling a baggie of pretzels out of his jacket pocket and shoving a handful into his mouth, "she's a *science* teacher. Get it? *Science?* Like, facts? Truth?" Crumbs spewed from his mouth as he spoke, and he held out the half-empty bag toward us. "Pretzel, anyone?" he asked, his mouth full.

"No, thanks," I told him, trying not to laugh at the crumbs stuck to his cheek.

"Dude," Toby said, sneezing again. "You have pretzels *all* over your face."

"Do I?" Will asked, wiping his cheek. He and Toby waved to me and Julian and turned the corner. "Gone now?" I heard him ask as their voices faded into the sounds of Gramercy Park on a sunny afternoon.

Julian and I walked together toward Union Square Park. Instead of going straight home like he usually did, though, he walked me to my building. "So, Central Park after school tomorrow?" I asked him.

He smiled. "Yup."

"And I'll call you tonight to compare math problems and to brainstorm for the assembly?"

"Yup," he said again.

The sun was filtering through the leaves of the trees, and despite everything terrible in the world, I felt better than I had in a while. I thought about capturing the moment in a paperweight—me and Julian standing there together on the sidewalk that was speckled in shadows and light. But it wasn't *exactly* the moment I'd want to have captured forever. Without thinking too hard about what I was about to do, I leaned forward and kissed Julian on the cheek. There. *That* was the moment I'd lower the orb over.

I've been hoping for the longest time that you'd do that, I imagined Julian saying. But he just grinned at me, bewildered, not saying a word.

"See you tomorrow, Julian," I told him, smiling, and went inside.

On the eighth floor, the elevator doors closed behind me and, as quietly as possible, I unlocked the front door. J.R. was where I thought he'd be, on the couch, sleeping beneath the crocheted blanket. I watched it rise and fall, rise and fall, until I was convinced that he was okay.

Then, from the kitchen phone, I dialed Bob's number at work like I'd promised I would, to assure him that J.R. was sleeping peacefully.

"When he's up, remind him to take five of the orange pills," Bob reminded me.

"I know," I whispered, not wanting to wake J.R.

"Maybe you'll be a doctor someday, Belly-ris," Bob told me.

"Nah, I'm a poet, not a scientist."

"Maybe you're both," he said.

I thought about that after hanging up the phone, and I thought of Ms. Staffio and how we'd all misjudged her. On the kitchen table was a green apple, the jar of peanut butter, and a sprig of mint leaves from the plant upstairs. I didn't think that J.R. had gone up to get it. He was too weak for that. Maybe he'd sent Mom to do it. Beneath the apple was a piece of notebook paper. I unfolded it. The handwriting was kind of faint, but it was still clear.

Bloom Like an Iris

A limerick by J.R. Holmes

April 20, 1987

There once was a young girl named Iris

Who came face-to-face with a virus

She allied herself

And her heart grew in wealth

And from anger, she bloomed like an iris.

I smiled. It wasn't bad for a limerick. I cut the apple and tapped my pencil against the tablecloth as I thought.

Calm Rage

A limerick by Iris Cohen

April 20, 1987

Where do I send this calm rage?

Trained lion, released from her cage.

Pacing the streets,

She'll never retreat.

Good thing she doesn't have mange.

The beginning of it was decent. The last line was definitely what Dad would have called lazy, but I didn't have much practice with limericks yet. Besides, rhyming was stupid, and I had things to do. I folded the poem and placed it quietly on the coffee table next to J.R.'s medicine and glass of water. Then I took out my math book and sat down in the chair across from him. I wanted to keep an eye on him. To watch the blanket move gently as he breathed. And I wanted to finish my homework so that when I was done, I'd have an excuse to call Julian.

Chapter Twenty

After school on Tuesday, Julian and I took the subway to Central Park. It was a perfect spring day, and the paths were swimming with people—joggers, couples holding hands, parents with children. They were living their lives, most of them likely unaware that all around them, people were dying of AIDS. It made me so sad to know that many of them would probably help, if they only knew how terrible this all was.

I sneaked a glance at Julian and imagined J.R. walking next to us instead of sleeping at home in the living room on the hospital bed that Bob had rolled in that morning. He would nudge me. *What are you waiting for, kid?* he'd ask, grinning. *Julian's a good guy. Talk to him.*

I smiled at the thought. "Julian?" I asked.

"Yeah?" he answered quickly, as if he'd been waiting for me to say something.

"Last time we were here, I had all these thoughts in my mind, and I didn't share any of them with you." I felt lighter. Sparkly.

"Really?" Julian asked. He looked at me eagerly as if he wanted to know more. Behind him, pigeons pecked at the pavement and a squirrel ran across a tree branch. A little girl walking with her mom dropped an ice-cream cone and started to cry.

"Yeah." I pictured J.R. again. In my image of him, his face was smooth and healthy, not hollow and pale. His gray curls swayed in the breeze. *And?* the image of him prodded, winking at me. "*And* I want you to know that I'm not strong like you think I am. I'm scared of what everyone thinks of me. I'm scared of what you think of me. I'm scared that if I tell you certain things, you'll think I'm weird and you won't like me anymore."

I want you to tell me everything, I pictured Julian saying. *I could never not like you.* I waited as he looked at his shoes, his cheeks pink. The image of J.R. waited, too.

Come on, I imagined J.R. mouthing in Julian's direction, gesturing wildly with his hands.

Finally, Julian looked at me confidently, as if he'd been emboldened by my openness. "I want you to tell me everything," he said. "I could never not like you."

J.R. jumped up and pumped his fist.

"Okay," I said eagerly, pointing to the entrance of the zoo. "I'm going to tell you the truth about why I didn't want to go to the zoo and why I'm never going there again."

"All right," Julian said, smiling.

My work here is done, J.R. said proudly. *I'm going home.* He took a couple of steps, fading into the scenery around us, then stopped. *Hey, kid, remember: I'm not dead yet.* I smiled and then turned back to Julian to tell him the story.

By the time that Julian and I had made our way to the Waldo Hutchins bench, I was exhausted from so much talking. I'd told him everything, from how I'd become friends with Mallory, Will, and Toby to the shock I'd felt when Dad had died, despite Mom's attempts to prepare me. I'd told him how every place I'd taken him last time we'd been in the park had been one of Dad's and my favorite spots.

We sat down on the bench in front of the Latin engraving. "Why didn't you tell me any of this last time we were here?" Julian asked.

"I don't know," I answered truthfully. An image of the sun-filled gallery at the Corning Museum of Glass parted the curtains of my mind and stepped into my consciousness. I remembered the sunshine, the glass windows, the glass display cases, and the dots of vibrant color surrounding me and J.R.

J.R.

I understood why Dad had loved him, and I remembered the way that my anger had transformed to sadness when he'd forced me to see what had been in front of me for so long: He was sick. He was dying. "I guess it was just too sad," I told Julian.

He nodded, and for a while, neither of us said anything.

"Do you ever think about how weird it is that two opposite things can exist at the exact same time?" he finally asked. "You can be totally nervous, but also calm. You can be really excited, but also scared."

"Yeah," I answered quickly. "Like, how can I be so sad and so happy at the same time?"

"I don't know," he answered. "It's really weird that we don't just, like, implode because of it."

I laughed, imagining that—imagining everyone around us who was feeling too many things all at once bursting into tiny fires and then transforming into piles of ash on the ground. Contemplating all that sadness and all that joy made me think of the ACT UP meeting and demos, and how all those feelings coexisted in the same place. And thinking about that brought to mind the assembly that the Philanthropy Club had planned with Ms. Staffio.

"We better get going," I told Julian. "We have those posters to make."

"Yeah, good point," he said.

"And I told my mom I'd be back by six. I'm watching over J.R. while she and Bob go on, like, a date or something."

Julian looked at me. "Are you okay with that?"

"Yeah," I answered quickly. I'd had a lot of time to adjust to Mom and Dad not loving each other in *that way*. "She seems happy when she's with Bob. He makes her seem like her old self."

Julian giggled. "Something just came to me," he said. "Let's say that they got married someday...." The thought was weird, but I supposed that it wasn't *too* terrible. "And they had a baby...." Now, *that* was weird. "And they named it Butt-ris."

I laughed. He was such a dork. "Meet our children," I added. "Eye-ris and Butt-ris."

Julian laughed, too.

"You know," I said. "When I first met you and you came to Philanthropy Club, I thought that you might be too cool for us."

"Nah," Julian replied quickly. "I'm a total nerd." He got up and unflinchingly reached for my hand. "Come on," he said, "let's go."

———

Back home, J.R. was awake in the hospital bed in the living room, propped up on pillows. Bob sat next to him, taking his pulse. I stayed quiet until he finished.

"Hi," I said from the doorway when Bob gently released his wrist. I searched J.R.'s face, trying to tell if he looked better or worse than he had when I'd left for school that morning.

"Hey, Head-ris," Bob said.

"Stop doing that, Iris," J.R. said in a raspy voice.

"Stop doing what?"

"Looking at me like you're trying to figure out how many days I have left."

"I wasn't," I lied, trying to smile. I knew he was kidding around, and I tried hard to hold on to both feelings at once—the sadness *and* the happiness. It was hard to do.

Mom came into the living room, her hair wet from the shower. "Hi, honey," she said, hugging me. "Did Bob give you instructions about the medication yet?"

"I'm just writing it down now," he said, getting up and handing me the notepad he'd been scribbling on.

I read his notes.

Instructions for Nurse Armpit-ris:
7 p.m.: 5.5 orange pills
9 p.m.: 1 white pill

Beneath the instructions were the name and phone number of the restaurant they'd be at—a new Mediterranean place near my school that they'd told me they'd been wanting to try.

Mom smoothed the thinning wisps of hair on Bob's

head, and as she did, I envisioned her paperweight heart brightening in her chest. What had been peach-colored for so long became vibrant sunset orange with brush-strokes of fuchsia. "Mom?" I asked suddenly. "You know the paperweights that Dad kept on his desk at work? Where'd they go?"

"They're in my bedroom," she said. "In my top drawer."

I nodded, stunned.

"Why?" she asked, noticing the shocked expression on my face.

"I just...I don't know," I said. "I didn't know where they went." It dawned on me that it was odd that I'd never asked her about them. "Can I get them?"

"Of course," she said.

"If anything seems amiss, don't hesitate to call us at the restaurant," Bob said as Mom handed him his jacket.

"Not dead yet!" J.R. rasped, and despite everything terrible, I smiled. I was so lucky and so unlucky.

"We won't be home much after nine," Mom added, kissing my cheek.

Once the door closed, I went to Mom's room, opened her top dresser drawer, and took out the paperweights.

J.R. had dozed off, and I put them onto the coffee table as I listened to him breathe. I felt so sad looking at them. All of those trapped colors. They were so beautiful and so breakable. Like Dad.

Then I pulled out the paper and markers that Ms. Staffio had sent me home with and got to work.

Chapter Twenty-One

On Wednesday, we finished up our posters and, with Ms. Staffio's permission, ran off copies at the Xerox machine in the teachers' lounge. By Thursday afternoon, I was jittery and anxious. Was this how the ACT UP organizers felt before the Wall Street demo? I imagined the energy that had hovered above me when I'd been at the center three weeks before. I tried to summon some of it to reappear over the school building.

At two fifteen, just as science ended, the intercom clicked on, and Principal Marshall's voice sputtered into the classrooms to call the students down to the gym, starting with the sixth graders. Ms. Staffio gave me, Julian, Will, and Toby a nod, and we rushed down ahead of the rest of our grade to get situated.

As Principal Marshall had promised when Julian, Will, Toby, and I had gone to him and Ms. Staffio with our proposal, the folding chairs faced the stage, where the projector screen was set up. In the center aisle, the film projector was ready to go. The room was empty aside from us, and I could hear the sixth graders approaching the doorways. The intercom clicked on again, and Mr. Marshall invited the seventh and eighth graders to the gym. I turned to my friends. I didn't know what to say. I wanted to thank them for being allies along with me, but it seemed cheesy to say that aloud.

"Hey," Will said, almost as if he was reading my mind, "we're here for you, but we're also here because we want to be."

"This is true," Toby declared.

I smiled at them. They were the biggest dorks, and they were my best friends. Then my eyes and Julian's connected. He nodded as if to agree with Will and Toby, but also to encourage me. *You're fine*, his eyes told me, and he seemed so sure about it that I decided to believe him.

"You ready to go?" Principal Marshall asked, walking into the gym alongside Ms. Staffio.

"I think so," I replied. Julian, Will, and Toby took their places in the front row, Toby holding the paper bag full of flyers with all kinds of slogans we'd come up with, like *HIV and AIDS: Know the Facts* and *Knowledge over Fear.*

"Let's get you set up on stage, then," Principal Marshall said. He was kind of a quiet guy, and I'd never thought much about him one way or another. But as he and I walked toward the stage, in a voice just above a whisper he said to me, "I quite respect you, Ms. Cohen. You know, my brother is gay. He lives in Boston. AIDS is taking out his community. What you're doing is good. The education piece, it's been missing. This is going to help."

I nodded at him, surprised.

A few days before, when I'd finally told Mom about Mr. Inglash and the splinter, she'd been shocked. "Mr. Marshall seemed so understanding when I talked to him about Dad back in March," she'd told me, exasperated. "I left the meeting feeling sure that I'd done the right thing for you. I'm so sorry, Iris."

Now that I'd gotten to know Principal Marshall a

bit better, I understood why she had thought that things would be okay. But if he knew that the "education piece" was missing, as he'd put it, why hadn't *he* fixed it? There were so many surprises and so many layers to everything around me. I didn't understand it all. I just knew that I needed to change things. For J.R., and for Dad.

The sixth graders had filled the seats closest to the stage by the time Ms. Staffio joined me at the podium, every hair in her tight bun in place, as usual. My grade was filing in through the back doors, and the eighth graders were behind them. Julian, Will, and Toby had gotten up, as planned, and were passing out the flyers we'd made. I studied Ms. Staffio's profile—her tortoise-shell glasses, wrinkled cheeks, and deep purple suit.

"Ms. Cohen," she said stiffly, still looking straight ahead. "Don't judge a book by its cover."

" 'Kay," I told her, shocked.

Then she hugged me right there on stage in front of the chaotic audience of kids taking their seats and waving their flyers in the air. "I lost my dad to a heart attack when I was your age," she told me. "You're much stronger than I was."

The bad feeling I'd had in the park with Julian washed over me, but this time I spoke up. "I'm not strong," I told her. "I care about what everyone thinks of me. I care about how they'll react to everything I'm going to say." My voice caught, and I cleared my throat. "I care *so much*."

She looked me in the eye. We were the same height, and I realized how piercing her dark eyes were. But then she smiled. "Ms. Cohen. Isn't that the point?" she asked me. "Isn't that the point of everything?"

Then she gave me a squeeze on the arm and left the stage.

I watched her go before turning to the audience. After a minute, they quieted down. My heart raced, and my legs quivered as I pulled the speech that Mom had helped me write out of my pocket, flattened it on the podium, and began to read.

"Hi," I said, and some people in the audience yelled "hello" in response before the teachers shushed them. Someone in the back row had made their AIDS flyer into a paper airplane and launched it into the crowd. I didn't know if they'd done it to be disrespectful, but the possibility emboldened me.

"I'm Iris," I went on. "Recently my dad died. He had AIDS."

The audience was totally silent now.

"When you hear 'AIDS,' you probably cringe, and there are lots of reason for that, which we're going to talk about today. One of the big problems with AIDS is that most people know nothing about it. Lots of people think you can catch it from sharing a bathroom with someone who has it, or drinking from the same drinking fountain, but neither of those things is true. I'm not a medical professional, obviously."

Some kids chuckled.

"With the support of Principal Marshall and the science department, especially Ms. Staffio, we've brought in a medical doctor from NYU to educate us on everything doctors and scientists currently know about HIV and AIDS. If you are educated, you don't have to be so afraid. Knowledge is power." I looked to the back of the gym, to where Mom and Ms. Staffio stood together, Mom's curls windblown and her scrubs wrinkled. "Please give a warm welcome to Dr. Cohen."

The audience clapped and turned to watch as Mom walked down the aisle and up the steps to the stage. She gave me a kiss on the cheek, and the audience laughed. Then I left the stage and sat down in the seat that Julian had saved for me as the lights dimmed, the projector flipped on, and Mom began to talk.

———————

Back home, I crept into the apartment quietly. Mom had given me a giant hug after the assembly, before rushing back to work. Julian, Ms. Staffio, and I had walked her to the front doors of the school as Ms. Staffio had gushed about how maybe she'd found her true calling. "Your style of interacting with the students is beautiful, Dr. Cohen," she'd said. "Just beautiful. Have you thought about offering this programing at other schools?"

I'd caught Mom's eye and raised my eyebrows at her as if to ask, *Yeah, Mom,* have you?

"Well, it's something to think about," Mom had said before hugging me again and running off to deliver more babies.

Now the apartment was quiet. J.R. was resting comfortably. He'd been alone for an hour and a half, since Bob had left for work. I didn't like the idea of him being on his own, but he seemed okay. Mom had let me know that Bob had given him something to help him sleep and that he'd be resting for a while.

The afternoon sun was dim in my bedroom. I turned on the lights and looked around. On my desk, next to Dad's navy binder, my red one, and the small pile of J.R.'s limericks, was the toppled picture frame that had fallen over when I'd slammed my door during the tantrum I'd had right after Dad had died. It was resting half on my well-worn copy of *Anastasia Krupnik*. I picked up the frame, careful not to cut myself on the shattered glass, and took out the photo of me, Mom, and Dad back before the divorce. We were in Central Park, sitting on the Waldo Hutchins bench, and I remembered Mom asking someone to take our picture. After, Mom had pointed to the Latin inscription. "Do you know what this means?" she'd asked.

It had never occurred to me before then to wonder about it, despite the fact that I'd looked at it so many times.

"No," I'd told her.

"One must live for another if he wishes to live for himself."

I thought about that now as I put the picture back into the glassless frame and carefully scooped the shards into the garbage can with the side of one of the binders. I thought of how it pretty much applied to everything in the whole world. Everything that mattered, anyway.

On my bedside table, next to my unmade bed, were the two paperweights that I'd taken from Mom's drawer. Our hearts: mine and Dad's.

I picked up the one that I'd always thought of as my heart.

Inside, eddies swirled in every shade of blue. Turquoise swoops became sapphire flames became the moment just before midnight navy. My heart was bubbles of glass within bubbles of glass, and all that blue was so sad, but the paperweight was also beautiful, especially where it was dotted with dewdrops of color: cherry pink, tranquil lime green, growing vines in red and yellow, and yawning flecks of peach. It was everything happy and everything sad, all at once; it was so many things to feel.

Next to it was Dad's heart. Inside, a turquoise spray of frozen-glass water hung over an untouchable, billowing, amber-orange ocean. Motionless raindrops touched petrified waves, and if you studied it closely, you could see two minuscule out-of-place specks of lemon yellow atop the sea. One had a thin, hairlike wisp above it, like a miniature light rising from a miniature lighthouse, and I pictured Dad there. He was pinprick-tiny, unreachable, suspended above the autumn sea. He was looking up at me. Smiling.

Earthworm, he whispered.

I picked up his heart and held it in my hands. Then I unfolded the ripped piece of notebook paper that had been waiting for me beneath it.

World Made of Glass
A limerick by J.R. Holmes
April 22, 1987

Who was this young girl, you ask,
Who had to grow up way too fast?
She learned as she grew
And, unblinking, walked through
This beautiful, breakable world made of glass.

AUTHOR'S NOTE

By 1987, when *World Made of Glass* takes place, approximately 500,000 people worldwide had died of AIDS. Unlike the early days of the COVID-19 pandemic, when the American public was aware of many of the facts surrounding the virus and the path it was taking, early on in the AIDS epidemic, facts and information were not widely known or publicized. There was no national or worldwide frenzy to understand HIV and AIDS or to help those being impacted. Most people diagnosed with HIV or AIDS were marginalized by society because they were gay men or intravenous drug users and, because of extreme bias against these marginalized groups, the government and pharmaceutical companies didn't feel an appropriate sense of urgency to prevent the spread of the virus or to help those who were sick. In fact, many people judged those who became ill with HIV and AIDS harshly, thinking that they were at fault for their sickness.

ACT UP was started by primarily white, financially stable gay men who were terrified of dying and furious about the ways in which HIV and AIDS were being ignored. As time went on, it became more and more diverse. By the end of the 1980s and into the 1990s, ACT UP was comprised of a racially diverse group of people of all genders, all socioeconomic statuses, and all kinds of backgrounds. Some were sick with HIV and AIDS, and some were their allies.

Dr. Anthony Fauci is mentioned a few times in *World Made of Glass*. As the book suggests, he and ACT UP had a complex relationship. In 1987, aside from AZT, which wasn't an effective or financially viable option for most people, taking illegal, experimental drugs was the only treatment option for people with HIV or AIDS. The primary reason for this was that there were very strict rules for how new drugs gained approval and how someone could get into a clinical trial for a new drug. At first, Dr. Fauci believed that the rules for entering these clinical trials should remain strict. As a result, people with HIV and AIDS didn't have legal treatment options, which is why you see the characters in *World Made of*

Glass taking black-market drugs and wondering whose side Dr. Fauci was on.

As time went on, Dr. Fauci reported that his empathy for people with HIV and AIDS grew. He recognized that, if he were in their shoes, he would have been fighting for his life just like they were fighting for theirs. In a *New Yorker* interview, he said, "I had to change." By the later 1980s, his relationship with ACT UP shifted. Eventually, at the urging of some of ACT UP's earliest members, Dr. Fauci supported relaxing some of the requirements for entering drug trials so that more AIDS patients could, through "parallel tracking," gain legal access to potentially helpful drugs rather than purchase them on the black market. This meant that once a drug was deemed safe, people could take it even though it hadn't been proven effective yet. Over time, Dr. Fauci came to collaborate regularly with members of ACT UP and, while his response to the epidemic isn't looked upon fondly by all early members, many of them came to respect him deeply and even consider him a close friend.

ACT UP's earliest days are described by its still-living members as energy-infused and vibrant, rageful, chaotic, and purposeful. In writing *World Made of*

Glass, I did my best to stay true to the complexity of these sentiments. I also tried to stay true to the most commonly used language to refer to groups of people at the time, which is why terminology such as *African American* and *homosexual* appear in the book. Every character in *World Made of Glass* is my own invention, but the vast majority of the book remains true to history. I did take artistic license to make minor adjustments in the following places:

• The TV and radio newscasts in *World Made of Glass* are fictionalized. In reality, the center and ACT UP were not in the news until after the Wall Street demo. However, the sentiments put forth in the news broadcasts are accurate. The information about Dr. Fauci is historically true, as are the facts regarding AZT and its approval. Fifteen percent of Americans were indeed in favor of forcibly tattooing people with HIV and AIDS as a way to identify them, and fifteen percent of the population supported forced quarantining.

• Both the Wall Street and Tax Day demos stay mostly true to history. Some details regarding the timing and location of the arrival of the police cars, trucks, and general police presence were altered slightly. Additionally, some of the chants were plucked from elsewhere on ACT UP's timeline and inserted into the Tax Day demo. It's important to note that the Tax Day demo was not one of ACT UP's more memorable or successful demonstrations. Unfortunately, it is remembered primarily for the police brutality that occurred there. There were no baggies of condoms or condoms slung from slingshots. At least, none that I know of.

• The ACT UP meeting that Iris attends stays mostly true to history. The racial diversity that she notices at the meeting would have been more reflective of an ACT UP meeting in the later eighties and into the nineties. In reality, nobody as young as Iris attended the meetings. Just as her mom told her, ACT UP *wasn't* for kids.

• While the medications mentioned in *World Made of Glass* are all actual drugs that were explored to treat HIV and AIDS, the details of J.R.'s medication, such as the color of the pills and experimental dosing, are fictionalized.

• Some details of the physical description of the Corning Museum of Glass are fictionalized to enhance the narrative.

• Iris's dad and J.R. were extremely privileged in that they were financially well-off and personally connected to powerful allies in the medical field. Their experiences didn't reflect the norm. While many AIDS patients died at home, the vast majority didn't have around-the-clock access to doctors, oxygen, or medication to help with their pain.

Several years ago, Sarah Schulman and Jim Hubbard interviewed over 185 of ACT UP New York's surviving members as part of the ACT UP Oral History Project. If you want to learn more about ACT UP, I highly recommend that you read these firsthand accounts at actuporalhistory.org. At the end of each interview, each interviewee is asked the same two questions: What was ACT UP's greatest accomplishment? What was its greatest disappointment? Dr. Rebecca Smith replies by saying, "There is one answer to both questions and that answer is the stories it allows us to tell. The greatest success is the stories it allows us to tell. The greatest failing is the stories it allows us to tell."

I hope that *this* story inspires young readers to react to injustices, whether they're present in their own lives or in the lives of others. I hope it inspires readers to search for hope and community in times of despair. And I hope it serves as inspiration for people to use their voices to act up and fight for justice.

ACKNOWLEDGEMENTS

A book

Cannot blossom in solitude. From seed to

Keyboard, so many people helped me. I could

Not have done it without ACT UP's Oral History Project:
    the voices

Of those who were there. Sara Rafsky, your reflections on your

World when your father, Bob Rafsky,

Lived and died were invaluable. Bill Goldstein, your expertise
    on Larry Kramer

Elucidated people and places. Wendy Schmalz, my agent and
    advocate, whose

Development was molded by the enormity of the AIDS
    crisis, I am

Grateful to know about your brother, Jeffrey Schmalz.
    His story opened my

Eyes to layers upon layers of complexity. *World*

*M*ade of Glass was received by LBYR with such enthusiasm.
    Thank you,

Especially to Lisa Yoskowitz, for everything you did to bring this

Novel to life. And

To the real Scott, rest in peace,

Sweet friend.

Special thanks to cover artist Ileana Soon and the entire Little, Brown Books for Young Readers team: Patricia Alvarado, Caitlyn Averett, Andy Ball, Danielle Cantarella, Sarah Chassé, Lily Choi, Jackie Engel, Shawn Foster, Anna Herling, Patrick Hulse, Sasha Illingworth, Alvina Ling, Annie McDonnell, Cara Nesi, Celeste Risko, and Megan Tingley.

Jessie Hearn

AMI POLONSKY

is a middle-school English teacher and the author of *Spin with Me*, *Threads*, and *Gracefully Grayson*. She lives outside of Chicago with her family and can be found online at amipolonsky.com.